Klepto

Lori Weber

James Lorimer & Company Ltd., Publishers
Toronto

© 2004 Lori Weber

First publication in the United States, 2004

James Lorimer & Company Ltd. acknowledges the support of the Ontario Arts Council. We acknowledge the support of the Government of Canada through the Book Publishing Industry Development Program (BPIDP) for our publishing activities. We acknowledge the support of the Canada Council for the Arts for our publishing program. We acknowledge the support of the Government of Ontario through the Ontario Media Development Corporation's Ontario Book Initiative.

The Canada Council | Le Conseil des Arts
for the Arts | du Canada

ONTARIO ARTS COUNCIL
CONSEIL DES ARTS DE L'ONTARIO

Cover design: Clarke MacDonald

Canada Cataloguing in Publication Data

Weber, Lori, 1959–
    Klepto / written by Lori Weber

(SideStreets)
ISBN 1-55028-837-7 (bound).—ISBN 1-55028-836-9 (pbk.)

I. Title. II. Series.

PS8645.E24K54 2004   jC813'.6   C2004-900481-6

James Lorimer	Distributed in the United States by:
& Company Ltd.,	Orca Book Publishers,
Publishers	P.O. Box 468
35 Britain Street	Custer, WA USA
Toronto, Ontario	98240-0468
M5A 1R7	
www.lorimer.ca	Printed and bound in Canada

To Ron and Cassandra,
who let me steal the time I needed
to write this book

Chapter 1

Shoplifting isn't hard to do, once you get the hang of it. It's easier than most people think. Actually, I'm kind of scared sometimes by just how easy it is. For me.

I'll give you an example. Consider it a kind of how-to manual: Shoplifting for beginners.

My best friend, Anita, plays the piano. Not that anyone would know this because she's so shy that she'll only play when no one is around, except me. She's really amazing. Her fingers just fly across the keys without missing or screwing up a note. I think she could be a superstar pianist one day, if only she could get over her stage fright.

Anita's parents have a lot of money so they can afford the lessons, but they get funny when it comes to buying sheet music. They'll put out for anything her piano teacher tells her to buy, but they won't let her have money to buy extra music that she wants to learn just for fun.

That's the big problem, the "just for fun" part. Anita's parents don't really believe in fun. So, if she wants to learn the music of say, Alanis Morissette, or even the Beatles, or some Broadway musical, like *Cats*, she has to use her allowance.

Last week, Anita and I went into the music store at the mall. Some of the books were stacked in the middle of the store, others were filed away in binders behind the cash. We spent a while flipping through books that were arranged by artist and type: jazz, pop, classical, folk. Anita picked up a *Women of the 90s* book, a real fat thing. It had hits by singers like Sarah McLachlan, Jann Arden, Melissa Etheridge, and others. Anita's a big fan of women's folk rock sort of music. The book's price was pretty fat too, forty-five dollars. She'd have to save her allowance for weeks and then never spend a penny in between. So, I picked up the book. I was cool. I didn't try to hide it. I held it to my chest like I wanted to buy it. That's the first rule. Never look secretive. Do everything in the open.

Then, we went up to the counter and Anita began to ask for classical pieces off a list her music teacher had given her. It sounded so impressive, the way she was spewing out names like Debussy and Bartok. We couldn't just be a couple of kids looking for trouble if one of us knew unusual names like that. I mean, they weren't your typical composers, like Mozart or Beethoven. Before long, a stack of sheet music was spread out on the counter in front of us. That's when I introduced this next crucial move. I said to Anita, "Don't you already have some of these? You better check, you know. You don't want to buy them for nothing." And then I smiled up at the old man behind the counter, a real Colgate, ear-to-ear smile, one that he couldn't help but be charmed by.

Next, Anita pulled a stack of music sheets out of her bag. In the meantime, just as I had hoped, the old guy moved off to serve someone else. We'd gained his trust by now, you see. There was no reason for him not to leave us alone. We knew our music. We were sweet. We didn't whisper. Never whisper! Then I picked up Anita's stuff and exclaimed loudly, "Oh ya, you did have this one. I told you. Good thing we checked."

The final move — you may have guessed it — was that while Anita was making a pile of sheet music to buy, I was being the helpful friend, putting her stuff back in her school bag while she made the purchase. Only, I had slipped in the *Women of the 90s* book, pushing it way to the bottom. I did it all slowly, deliberately, looking up and around like I didn't mind being seen.

When the buckle of Anita's school bag clicked shut, that feeling hit me, just like it always does. It's a feeling like none other I've ever had, a rush of energy that surges through my whole body, like I've been plugged in. My skin tingles and I have to suppress an urge to scream. That's always the moment when I could blow it.

Anita was still getting her change and the old

guy was slipping the sheet music into an elegant white bag with a treble clef design on its front. And I just wanted to yell at them to hurry the hell up, and then run, run for the door and out of the mall, whooping and hollering. But, of course, I didn't. You have to maintain control to the very end.

What I will describe next is my master touch, the *pièce de résistance* of my performance. I stopped ever so casually by the stacks where we had looked earlier and said, in an ultra-friendly voice, "Maybe next time you'll be able to afford the *Women of the 90s* book, Annie." You'll notice I didn't use her real name, another golden rule. A thrill ran through me when I said this. I mean, what kind of idiot would suspect a kid who could stand there and say that so coolly after just having stolen the very book she was talking about?

See, I told you. Easy, right?

Chapter 2

My mother is redecorating — again! It's become an obsession with her. She has redone three rooms since my older sister, Hannah, left in July. First, she painted the living room, then she retiled the kitchen floor. Last month I spent a whole useless day helping her glue seashells onto the bathroom wall.

Today, she's changing the wallpaper in the dining room. Right now she's perched at the top of a stepladder, wetting down the old paper with a sponge and then pulling it off in long strips, like streamers. She rips with such gusto, as though she's stripping away something that she really hates.

"Wow, look at this one," she says, holding up a piece that runs from ceiling to floor. It reminds me of when my sister and I were little and we'd compete to see who could find the longest french fry at McDonalds. We called them "wumps." We'd pull them out of the bright red box and let them dangle over our mouths before chomping on them.

"Come on, Kat. You said you'd help," my mother calls out.

"No, I didn't." Does she really think I have nothing better to do on a Saturday? Even my father has vanished for the day.

"Well, I'm asking you to, please."

My mother never used to fuss around the house. She preferred to do meaningful things with her time, like starting a co-op daycare. She did that with our neighbour, Toby, whose son, Andy, was my best friend when I was four. And she never cared about mess. Once we'd started school, she let us bring friends home for lunch whenever we wanted. We'd turn the kitchen inside out, but she didn't mind. She said a home wasn't for show but for living in, so dirt didn't matter. When I look at her now I can't believe she ever said that.

"God, are we expecting the Queen or something?" I ask. My mother's face falls and, of course, I feel bad. Sometimes I forget that she has to be protected because she's still fragile over Hannah's leaving. But our house is changing so fast, I don't feel like it's mine anymore. What if she's working her way toward my room? I might not be able to stop her. Sometimes I feel that I have no control over anything that happens under this roof anymore, and it scares me.

"No, we're not expecting the Queen, but you do know who is coming this week? I don't need to remind you, do I?"

God, no. How could I forget? It's Miss Corvette — the social worker. She comes every second Wednesday to give us an update on whether Hannah's making any progress in her new home, as if I care. Every night, when I go to bed, I look across at my sister's empty bed and try to picture her in the group home. I see a long dormitory, with rows of beds up either side. When the caretaker turns out the lights, I see the girls spring out of bed and gather in the middle. Here, they share whatever forbidden objects they've managed to steal — cigarettes, the odd joint, some booze. Then, they share stories of all the illegal activities that brought them together. I picture them feeding each other a midnight snack of rage and rebellion. I can't imagine how this could lead to transformation.

"Here. You sponge," my mother calls out. A wet sponge hits me in the stomach, snapping me back to the present. The bottom of the walls, where the wallpaper is still stuck, looks like a pattern of tall, wild grass. I kind of like it like this. It's exotic.

"Why don't we leave it like this? It's cool. It looks like a jungle." I want to add that a jungle would suit our home these days, but don't.

"Kat, please, just strip, will you?"

There's no point in trying to joke around with my mother anymore. She hasn't been light-hearted for ages. It must have been in another lifetime that she put on some of her old Diana Ross records and we choreographed the songs, with my mother taking the lead role and my sister and me playing the Supremes. The serious expression on her face tells me that she won't rest until the new wallpaper is up. She'll put all her energy into measuring it precisely and hanging it so that not a single bubble of air is left alive. It will be neat and impeccable.

Everything that our family currently isn't.

Chapter 3

Anita's house is ten times bigger than mine. It sits right on the corner of a dead-end street, elevated on a little hill. I bet Anita's father had the builders shape the hill on purpose before construction began. He would have wanted the house up high, so that he could look down on all his neighbours.

It's not impossible that he's got that kind of clout. After all, he owns tons of land and his own construction company. There are whole plots of undeveloped land around the neighbourhood that have his company's name on them, painted two metres high on For Sale signs. Because his office is in the basement, it's Anita's actual home phone number that is broadcast everywhere, for all the world to see. I know this embarrasses her, but Anita's father's too cheap to put in a second line. One of these signs sits just across from our high school in a wooded lot.

"Hey, isn't that your number Anita? Hey guys,

for a good time, call 555-5407 — Anita will take you up to Heaven." John Fish started this chant back in grade seven. You wouldn't think that someone with a pathetic last name like Fish would be so brazen. Anita should be used to the chant by now, but she isn't. She turns beet red every time, especially since the guys all crack up after John says it. Anita isn't what you'd call a babe. She's a bit on the heavy side.

I take a deep breath before ringing Anita's bell. I know her mother will answer, because she always does. And she'll most likely have a dish-towel in her hands. Either that or a pair of knitting needles, her out-of-the-kitchen pastime.

"Hello, Kathleen." Anita's mother refuses to call me Kat. I've been called Kat for as long as I can remember, mostly because I come from a long line of Kathleens on my father's side — his mother and her mother and so on.

"Hi, is Anita in?" I have to say this every time, even though we both know why I'm here.

"Yes, she is. Come in."

"Thanks." Anita's mother stands aside to let me in, then waits while I take off my shoes. I can feel her tall, narrow body behind me. When my shoes have been placed perfectly straight on the mat, she tells me to go ahead.

Anita's in the basement, making great progress on the new music we "picked up" the other day. She's playing "Angel" by Sarah McLachlan. She has to have another music book ready to cover it up, in case her mother comes down. Whenever she does, she stands at the doorway, arms folded across her chest, nodding her approval. I always get the feeling that she's unmoved by the music; she's judging Anita with her brain, probably hoping that they're not wasting their money on a no-talent. It's pretty much the same with Anita's father. He stays in his office beyond the sliding wood doors at the end of the room. It's forbidden territory and Anita swears he'd kill her if he ever caught her in there.

"That sounds great. God, I can't believe you can actually make any sense of all those dots and squiggles. It's amazing," I say, trying to encourage her.

Anita just shrugs. "Do you want to go somewhere?"

"It's up to you. I could just hang out if you want to keep practicing." I'm just glad to have escaped the wallpapering.

"No, I'd rather go out. We'll have to think up somewhere to tell my mother, though." Anita's mother doesn't consider just going out a worthwhile activity. We need a destination. We could tell her the library, she'd like that, but what's the point? If she knew Anita had to do some research, she'd ask why she wasn't using the Internet. It must have been easier to get away from home before the world became so high-tech. Anita's mother even bought her a pager. The teachers tell us to keep cellphones and pagers turned off in class, so Anita has to keep hers on vibrate, in case her mother has to contact her in an emergency. I can't imagine what the emergency would be. The oven isn't working? The fridge light is out?

"Tell her we're going to the mall, to window shop." That's where we'll probably end up anyway. There isn't really much else to do in our neighbourhood. Besides, I love the mall. Everything is perfect there. There are no holes in the walls, no scratches on the paint, no leaks in the ceilings. None of the glass fronts of the stores are cracked. None of the millions of wires that carry the electricity and run the phones and web hookups show. The tiles shine so brightly you can almost look down and use them for mirrors. The plants in their huge pots reach up to the sunlight so energetically you almost expect them to start dancing right in front of your eyes. The gold, silver, and chrome fixtures sparkle. It's as though everything in the mall is coated in some magic substance that keeps it totally immune to the dirt people carry in from the outside world. Even the silver garbage cans shine.

Upstairs, Anita's mother is pulling a tray of muffins out of the oven. I can tell she doesn't approve of our outing — too aimless — but at least she doesn't try to stop us. Her face is all stern and pinched when she tells Anita to be home for supper at six.

Anita waits until we're around the corner and off her street before lighting a cigarette. She's been smoking like crazy lately. And when she's not smoking, she's always checking that her pack is within reach, like a security blanket.

I look back toward Anita's house, half expecting some kind of searchlight or loudspeaker to come out of the roof.

But there's nothing, just the quiet street. Nothing stands between us and the mall.

Chapter 4

Monday morning I wear the sweater I "bought" at the mall on Saturday. I absolutely love it. It's powder blue with three red stripes around the bottom and it's made of a kind of shiny, velvety yarn.

I'm standing around with Anita at break, on a little side street where groups of kids gather. The people who live here are always complaining to the principal about the noise we make and the garbage we leave behind. Every now and then we get a lecture about learning to respect public property and how would the world look if everyone just threw their garbage into the streets, blah, blah, blah. But it doesn't stop us. And the teachers on duty can't exactly follow a thousand students around, can they?

"I love your sweater, Kat," Jess calls over. Although we've been going to the same school since kindergarten, Jess and I have never spoken more than a few words to each other. Jess and her friend Emma were always the most popular girls in school. They were the first to wear eyeshadow in grade six. And in grade seven they were sent home to change out of their belly-showing tops into more modest clothing. Anita and I have always secretly called them air-headed fashion-girls, the type we'd never want to be.

"Where'd you get it?" says Jess.

"At the mall."

"Wow, I love it too," says Emma. She and Jess come over and start touching my sweater to see if it feels as soft as it looks.

"How much did it cost? It must have cost a fortune."

"Well, actually …" I hesitate a little, because only Anita knows about my hobby. I only did it for the first time this summer, in July. "I didn't buy it."

"Was it a present? You're so lucky."

"No, I … I stole it," I whisper. I imagine the old people who live in the house behind the hedge eavesdropping for things to report us on. Anita stays perfectly calm, while the other two gasp.

"You bitch! You're kidding!? Oh my God. How? How did you do it? Like, how did you not get caught?"

"Well, if you know the right places, it's not so hard." This was one of those discount clearance stores where all kinds of merchandise is heaped in big bins. You really have to dig down and rummage to find the good stuff. The dressing rooms were unattended, well, except for a tired-looking woman who was busy carting out clothes people had left behind.

"Wow, you have nerve!" says Emma.

I just shrug and try to wear an "it's no big deal" expression on my face, but it's not easy. I'm remembering how yesterday, as I was stuffing the sweater under the back of my loose top, I almost lost my nerve. I knew that the woman guarding the dressing rooms would be distracted, but I couldn't be sure she wouldn't notice the slight bulge at my back. This was the riskiest theft I'd ever undertaken. You see, I'd stuffed one sweater inside another before going into the dressing room so that I'd have something to hand back. Even that had been risky because I had to do it in the open, in the middle of the store.

"I'd never have the nerve," Emma continues. "You've got guts."

"Do you ever!" adds Jess. They're both staring at me in amazement, as if they're seeing me for the first time. Normally, they both look right through me as if I don't exist.

"It's no big deal," I say, although I'm beginning to wonder if I made a mistake telling them, because their mothers know my mother. This morning I had carried the new sweater to school in my knapsack and changed here, although I doubt my mother would've noticed that the sweater was new anyway. Sometimes I think she's living on another planet. Her eyes will be on me, but she isn't seeing me. She hears me speak, but I can tell she isn't listening.

I'm kind of relieved when the bell rings. Anita grinds out her cigarette, her third, under her running shoe. We walk back in silence, but every now and then I catch Jess and Emma staring over at me as if they're trying to figure me out.

And then there's Andy, coming up fast behind us. He smiles and gives me a little wave when I look back at him. God, I hope nobody else saw that. I've never really had a boyfriend. Of course, Jess and Emma have. They're always giggling and tossing their hair when guys are around. Sometimes, at break, they just stand there with their arms wrapped tightly around their boyfriends' bodies.

I could never picture myself doing that with Andy.

"Hi, Kat," Andy says when he catches up to me on the stairs. "What did Jess want?" He screws his nose up when he asks this, as though Jess is smelly.

"Nothing," I answer curtly. I can't stand the thought of Andy knowing about the sweater. It would be too close to home. After all, he is my neighbour. And he used to be my best friend when we were little. I sometimes think he still thinks we're best friends even though I never pay him any attention anymore. He's always looking over and smiling at me in class, as if we have plans to go off and play together after school. I wish he'd get over it.

"Well, bye," I add quickly, before he can ask any more questions. Then I run up ahead to catch up with Anita.

Chapter 5

Miss Corvette looks like a business woman. I suppose that's what she is. Except she doesn't deal with merchandise. She deals with children's lives, moving them from place to place to get the best profit. Her fingernails are so perfect, they're scary. When she raises her cup I study them. They're filed to perfect arches, even the pinky, and painted a subdued pink. If any cuticle even thinks of crawling up those nails it'll be scraped off before it has a chance to finish the thought. Those aren't nails that tear off wallpaper or scrub toilets. She must have a maid. Or, if she's married, maybe her husband does all the housework. I don't know if she's married or not, though, because that's the funny thing about social workers. They get to know you inside out but you don't get to know them at all. They sit there and ask prying questions, but they keep themselves all locked up like their gray suits are vaults.

"So, how are you all?" Miss Corvette opens the conversation, now that the adults have tea and I have a can of pop. A plate of cookies sits on the coffee table, untouched. It'll probably stay that way, like last time.

"Fine," says my mother, flatly. She worked frantically all morning finishing the dining room walls and she actually made me vacuum the sofa when I got home from school today. It's as though she thinks our house is under scrutiny when Miss Corvette is here and that she'll be checking it out to see whether it lives up to the standard necessary for the return of one troubled teenager.

My father just grunts. He's sitting on a hard-backed chair, as though he doesn't want to get too comfortable.

"And you, Kat?" Miss Corvette fixes her mascaraed eyes on me. This part must be in her training manual. Rule number 25: make everyone in the home feel included. I nod, as if to say I agree with my parents. We're all fine. Peachy. Not a care in the world. Just as you'd expect when the eldest kid in the family has been taken away because she was making the house a living hell.

"Well. Things are continuing pretty much as before. Hannah seems to be adjusting well. She's into the routine. Routine is often really important, you know. There are rules all the girls have to follow, and she seems to be following them well." Does Miss Corvette mean to imply that Hannah was lacking routine at home? That my parents didn't set enough rules? After my sister was taken away, I overheard my father tell my mother that he never wanted to be the heavy with his kids. He wanted to be their friend first. He wondered if maybe this had been a mistake.

"No problems to report from the school either. She's in class, doing the work," Miss Corvette continues. I almost gasp. This doesn't sound at all like Hannah.

My father clears his throat, as if he's going to speak, but then changes his mind. He's just staring at his hands, circling his thumbs. I find it hard to believe that he's a guidance counsellor and that he spends his days listening to teenagers share their problems. He looks too burdened. He didn't always look this way, though. He used to be the kind of father other kids envied. He always volunteered at school to help out with Pedestrian Rallies and Bike-a-thons and school plays, things that mostly mothers volunteered for. On Career Days, when parents are invited in to talk about their jobs, my father always drew the biggest crowd. He didn't wear a three-piece suit and hand out business cards. He came in jeans and a sweatshirt and got the kids to sit in a circle cross-legged on the floor. He sat right down there with them, not worrying about getting dirt on his butt.

This year, he said he was too busy to come in for Career Day. I know that was just a lie. He was just too busy worrying about Hannah to bother.

"Can she come home to visit?" my mother

finally asks. No one in the family has seen Hannah for two months, since mid-July.

"Yes, maybe soon. But now that she's getting so well established, it might be best to just let her continue to settle in. We don't want anything to unsettle her now."

My father's a pacifist, and yet I can almost feel him wanting to leap from his chair and smash Miss Corvette's head.

My mother doesn't challenge Miss Corvette's logic either. It's as though she has completely given over the care of her first-born child to this stranger, to this person who must know better than her because my mom just made a mess of things.

"Well, I'll stop by again in a while. And you can phone me, anytime. I think everything will be all right. Really, I do." Rule number whatever: always leave the family with a scrap of hope.

"I baked some cookies. Can you get them to her?" my mother asks as Miss Corvette stands up.

"Sure. I'd be happy to. It would be good for her to receive a gift from home." Miss Corvette looks down at me when she says this. She's been suggesting for weeks that I write to my sister. She says it might mean a lot to her to know that I'm thinking about her. That I miss her.

But I was never any good at lying. Not like that.

Chapter 6

My parents are going to visit my sister tonight, in about an hour. Miss Corvette called last night and said that Hannah had asked to see them. My mother wanted Hannah to come to the house, but Miss Corvette said that Hannah wasn't ready to come home yet, not even to visit. So my parents are going to the group home. Miss Corvette said this way Hannah would feel less threatened because they would be on her turf. I know all this because my parents went over the whole conversation for hours last night, raking through it as if hidden messages were buried underneath, waiting to be unearthed. And they're still going over it now.

I'm sitting at the dining room table trying to get started on my English composition. The topic is the very best family vacation. I was daydreaming in class so I don't know if this means one that my family has really taken, or what my ideal family vacation would be. Either way, my mind is completely blank.

"What did she mean — less threatened?" my father wants to know. "I mean, when did we ever threaten her? When have I ever threatened my children? I've never even raised my voice to them." He could look over at me for confirmation of this. But my father doesn't look to me for anything. I'm invisible to him, now that Hannah has called.

"She didn't mean anything by it. Don't get in a twist," my mother says, trying to calm him.

"And what's this business about her turf? Is this a gang war or something? Hannah always knew this was her home, her turf. We never made her feel otherwise. We've always respected our kids' privacy. We never even go into their room. That social worker is twisting everything up. Don't think I don't know that game. She's waiting for us to confess something. That's easier than fixing the child. I know what she's doing. After all, I'm in the business too, you know?" My father is pacing the length of the kitchen now.

Suddenly, the dream vacation comes to me. My parents and sister strapped to the outside of a missile, blasted off into outer space. And me left behind to a blissful, peaceful house where I can do what I want, when I want. Not that I'm not pretty much left alone now. But the air would be fresher, less stale, less tainted by Hannah.

"Look, calm down," my mother pleads. She's

probably worried that my father will wear a groove in the new tiles.

"It's psychobabble, gobbledygook! That's what it is. Her own turf and space and all that — on her terms. Empowering the child. Making her feel like she's in control. I mean, Christ, we never took control of her, ever." My father's voice lifts as if he's asking a question, one that can't be answered.

I can vouch for that. No one was ever in control but Hannah. She could scream louder and slam a door harder than any of us. She could muster up a strong argument in support of later hours and more allowance. From day one, she seemed to know that our father was a big, soft teddy bear. He was the heroic draft dodger who'd come to Canada thirty years ago to avoid being drafted into the US army and sent off to Vietnam to kill people he had nothing against. In old pictures he's weighted down by peace symbols strung on leather shoe-laces around his neck, holding signs with slogans like "Make love, not war."

When the front door clicks shut I realize that my parents never even bothered to say goodbye. I crumple up my paper. Forget family vacations! What I need right now is a vacation from my family.

Especially now that Hannah is starting to creep back into it.

I remember the last time my parents hurried out the door without saying goodbye, except that day, Hannah went with them.

It was the beginning of summer. Hannah was

supposed to be at work at the Tim Horton's up on Boulevard Saint-Jean. At least that's where my father dropped her off every morning on his way to work. At about ten o'clock the phone rang. It was Hannah's boss. He was this guy who Hannah knew from school. All I said was hello and then he went off on this long rant, asking me where I'd been for the last two weeks and yelling how he couldn't keep covering for me, even if we were friends, and what the hell was I trying to do, get him fired? You see, he thought I was her. When he finally realized his mistake, he said "Oh, shit" and hung up.

And I was left with the terrible decision of whether to tell.

I remembered other discovered deceptions, like the false address to the party. That time, my father left home at midnight to find Hannah. She was supposed to be home at eleven. The address led him nowhere, but he drove around until he found her. She was at a wild party that was in full swing in a flat above a store. My father had to walk over kids passed out on the stairs to get to her. Hannah was so out of it, she laughed for an hour on her bed afterwards. We all listened, stunned.

There were other examples, enough to make me think twice about telling. That night at dinner, my parents were praising me because I had received a certificate in the mail for being on the grade eight honour roll. Suddenly Hannah leaped out of her chair and threw her water in my face, as if I was a fire she wanted to put out. She called me a goody-two-shoes, little Miss Bloody Perfect and a few other complimentary things.

That's when I blurted it all out. I recounted the phone call and hurled my accusations, as if each one was a sharp piece of cutlery.

In the middle of our shouting, the doorbell rang and we looked out the porch window to see two police officers standing there, shifting their weight from foot to foot. At first, I thought a neighbour had heard the fight and called in a noise disturbance, but it turned out the police were looking for Hannah. After they left with my parents and sister, I called Anita and begged her to try to get out. I had to go to the mall. I had to be someplace shiny and neat and understandable.

That was the first day I stole something. I left the house knowing that I was going to do something different that day, something so big that it would make me a different person. It would take me across a line that I could never cross back over. I wasn't even careful. I did it by instinct. I ripped a red bandana off a hook, scrunched it into a ball inside my fist and walked out. My heart was pounding as I ran down the escalator. I could see Anita leaning over the railing above me, looking confused. I ran all the way to the washroom and released my fist only when I was safely locked in a stall. I could hardly remember what I'd taken. A red bandana, something I would never wear, that would have cost me only $1.99.

When the realization of what I had done hit me, I was amazed. Stealing had been easy. I knew I could do it again, only next time I'd take something more valuable.

Chapter 7

At breakfast next morning, nobody mentions the visit with Hannah. If my parents are waiting for me to bring it up, they're in for a long wait. I don't want to know. I just want to gobble down my toast as fast as possible and get to school. If they've had any kind of happy reunion they can reminisce on their own. I barely call out goodbye from the door. But neither of them looks up anyway. They're off in Hannah-land.

I spend the day going through the motions of school: History, Geography, Math, French, and English. I never did write the family vacation composition that is due today. I grumble some excuse and promise to have it for Monday. Mr. Curtis gives me an "I don't know what's gotten into you" kind of look but tells me he'll accept it then but not a day later.

After school, I ask Anita if I can go to her house, but she thinks her mother won't like it because she has homework and piano practice.

"Please, I don't want to go home."

"Why not?"

"'Cause. There's no point. My parents will just want to talk about my sister."

"Oh." Anita knows all about Hannah. But she's the only one, apart from Andy, and he only knows because of what my mother told his mother. No one else at school knows that I have a sister who's living in a group home for troubled kids because she was caught delivering drugs. I found out when I got home from the mall the day I stole the red bandana. Skipping out on work was the least of Hannah's transgressions. Instead of working, she'd been hanging out at some older guy's apartment. One of her friends was sort of going out with him. He'd let a gang of them just hang around all day, smoking up and watching TV. He'd order pizzas and let them use his Jacuzzi. But eventually he began putting them to work. He'd give them little packets of hash and grass to deliver around the neighbourhood. Of course, he eventually got busted and squealed on his little helpers, Hannah included. I've never seen this guy, but I picture him as an older guy with a whiskered face and long thin hair pulled back into a ponytail. He's sitting on a tattered armchair, his pot-belly sticking out, ordering Hannah and her friends around. How could anyone, even Hannah, be that stupid?

"Well, aren't you even a little bit curious about what happened at the home?" Anita asks.

"No, I don't want to know. All I know is that our house is much more livable without her. There's no more fighting, no more dramatic blow-ups. That's all I care about now."

"If I had a sister, I'd at least want to know how she's doing," Anita says, looking at her shoes.

"I know how she's doing. Her social worker keeps telling us. And you just say that because you don't have a sister. You don't know how lucky you are that you don't, either. My sister has only made my life miserable."

Anita gives me a cold look. I know what she's thinking. She's thinking about the kind of sisters you read about in books, like *Little Women* or *Little House on the Prairie*. Not the kind of sisters who swear and throw things at each other, things that hurt like hair brushes and mugs. She never had to live with a sister who would come home late at night and shake you awake in your bed and tell you she hated you and was going to kill you. She didn't know what it was like to sleep with one eye open on the bed across the room, watching your drugged-up sister twist and jerk as though she was doing battle with an invisible dragon.

In fact, Anita doesn't really know what it's like to be related by blood to anyone. She has no siblings. And, she's adopted. Her real mother gave her up at birth. Anita barely knows a thing about her mother, except that she was French.

"Please, Anita. You can sneak me in and I'll sit there quiet as a mouse and you can practice your piano. What's your mother going to do? Throw me out?"

"Okay, but don't blame me if she does."

Anita's mother raises her eyebrows in disapproval when she sees me. Anita tells her we're going to study and her mother pinches her lips together as if she doesn't believe it. "Make sure you practice your piano too, dear," she says. Then she settles back onto her stool and picks up her knitting. Some really bright orange wool is nestled in her lap. A few rows of whatever she's knitting hang from the thick silver needles. It looks like she's knitting herself a pumpkin for Hallowe'en. She strings the yarn around her index finger and pokes the needle into the first stitch. Then she looks right up at me, straight into my eyes.

"Are you coming?" Anita calls. I nod yes, but I can't make my feet work. Not with her mother piercing me with her eyes. Finally, I blink and walk away, turning into the bathroom beside Anita's room. Its fixtures are all gold and shiny and a Jacuzzi that's bigger than my bed is sunk into the corner. I look into the gilded mirror above the sink. I stare into my eyes to try to see what Anita's mother might have seen. But I don't see anything unusual. It was just that woman, trying to unnerve me.

Before leaving, I notice a wicker shelf in the corner. On it sits a glass dish filled with scented soaps in the shape of sea-shells. I grab three soaps and stuff them into my pocket. I hope Anita's mother can smell their perfume when I pass her on the way out.

Chapter 8

Mr. Curtis is handing back the English composi-
tions. My head is down on my desk and all I want
to do is curl up and snooze. I've been staying up
late because my parents have had several evening
meetings with Hannah and Miss Corvette at the
group home. I remember our first meeting with
Miss Corvette in her office downtown back in
April, months before Hannah got sent away. We
were there because Hannah and her so-called
friends had been caught breaking into gym lockers and stealing jewelry and watches. This visit
with the social worker had been set up by the
school's principal and guidance counsellor, someone my father knew from work. He said having to
attend it was like a fireman watching other people
put out a fire in his own house.

The four of us sat on two sofas and Miss
Corvette sat at her desk between us, trying to
mediate. But there wasn't much to mediate since

no one wanted to talk. At one point, she looked straight at me and said, "Kathleen, can you tell your sister how you feel about her?"

I was stunned, frozen. My sister. I didn't know where my sister had gone. She'd been replaced by this wild girl, who even now was letting an unlit cigarette dangle in defiance between her lips, who never looked at me anymore without glowering, as though she wanted to hit me. Who had hit me, hard, with a closed fist, because I took too long in the bathroom one morning.

"Do you love her?" Miss Corvette then asked, saying the sentence in a way that sounded rehearsed.

The best I could do was shrug. I was torn. I wanted to say yes, because that was partly true. But I wanted to scream that no, I didn't love her. I hated her with all my might. Because that was true too.

* * *

"Kat, excellent composition, even if it was late. Would you like to read it to the class. please?"

I start to shake my head no, but Mr. Curtis has one hand on the back of my chair, pulling it out, and is indicating the front of the class with his free hand. I look over to Anita for support. After all, it was her piano playing that inspired the composition that day I took refuge at her house. She was practicing some gentle, mesmerizing piece that sent me back to that trip to Prince Edward Island eight years ago. Anita's head is down, probably in sympathy,

37

since speaking in front of the class makes her sick. Only Andy's face, there in the front row, is sending me some encouragement.

My fingers are shaking so badly the paper is rattling. I read on automatic pilot, trying to dissociate myself from the words, as though someone else wrote them, as though this is merely a description of a movie, or a sappy tissue commercial. I give the characters completely different faces and read in a flat, monotonous voice.

My Ideal Family Vacation

My ideal vacation would be a trip to Prince Edward Island, the home of Anne of Green Gables. The Atlantic Ocean glistens like a sea of jewels beneath the ferry and the island is a shiny red gem in the distance. As we get closer, the tall grasses gently wave us on, as if they've been expecting us.

Our white wooden cottage sits just a few feet from the ocean. All night long we hear the waves lapping against the shore. Every morning after breakfast we take a long walk along the beach, sinking our feet into the red sand, collecting sea shells and speckled rocks in our buckets. The seagulls are so tame they don't flutter away when we approach, they merely screech their hellos into the wind.

Afternoons we play in the water. We have lots of inflatable rafts, but we're careful not to drift too far out. When the tide is out, we take big sticks and draw in the sand. Cats become our specialty. We draw whole colonies of cats from one end of the cove to the other. Then we sit back and watch the tide come back in, drowning our creations. We pretend to be devastated and fake cry into our towels.

Some days, we hike back into the tall, tall grasses and make houses by rolling around and flattening grass into rooms. We sneak out tea and cookies and invite each other over for afternoon tea. Our tabletops are big stones found by the water. We are Anne and Diana, having tea and acting so grown up, only ours is real tea and not currant wine that makes one of us sick.

In the evening, we climb a little hill, to a spot where a couple of rope swings have been tied to maple trees. From here, we can see way out into the ocean. The ships are smaller than our pinkies and tiny fishing boats bob on the surface like corks.

At night we make a fire of sticks on the beach and roast marshmallows, slapping our skin lazily every now and then to keep the mosquitoes away. Sometimes, in an eerie way, we both start singing the same song at the exact same time, letting our voices rise up over the smoke.

We sleep curled up side by side in the same bed, our breath shaking each other's hair. We dream the same dreams, as though the pictures travel through our linked arms into each other's sleep. In the morning we sometimes awaken to find our fingers entwined like stalks of grass.

We are best friends, kindred spirits. Sisters.

By the end of the story, I can no longer control the lump in my throat. I can't believe I'm about to cry in front of the entire grade nine class, John Fish included.

I run out of the room and know, just like the day I stole the bandana, that my life will never be the same again.

I hear a chair scraping on the floor behind me, and turn to see Andy getting up. Andy is the last person I want to see now, so I protect myself by running into the girls' bathroom. I know he'd never have the nerve to enter it.

Chapter 9

I can't go back to school today, not after that freak show. The whole class will be waiting to tear me apart. I can just hear Jess and Emma mocking me, with John Fish leading the pack. A crybaby in grade nine!

Last night, I arranged to skip school today and head downtown with Anita. I had to talk her into it on the phone for an hour first. Anita's parents would kill her if they found out, but I've thought of a surefire way that they won't.

We leave our respective houses as usual and meet at Dupuis, to catch the bus. Since it's rush hour we don't have to wait long. Half an hour later, at the Lionel-Groulx Metro station, the doors open and everyone gets off. Anita and I become part of the swarm trudging down the steps, along the path, through the steel doors and down the long escalator to the Metro platform. I love being swept along by the crowd and not having to decide which way to go. I wish I could keep doing it for the rest of the year.

It's about nine o'clock when we get downtown. The stores aren't open yet, so we pop into the food court at the Eaton Centre and share a muffin and orange juice. Anita smokes half a dozen cigarettes.

"Is there any particular reason why you're smoking so much lately, Anita?" I've been wanting to ask her this for ages.

Anita shrugs. "I'm not."

"Yes, you are."

Anita shrugs again. "I have a lot on my mind."

"You do? Like what?" Anita's always been a bit like a nut that's hard to crack.

"I've been thinking a lot about something lately."

I keep quiet to encourage her to go on, but she's clammed up again.

"Something ... like what?"

"I want to try to find my real mother," she blurts out.

I don't know what to say. Anita's only mentioned the fact that she's adopted once, after she won the French prize when we graduated from elementary school. Anita said that her real mother had at least given her something useful. I didn't understand, until she explained that her biological mother was French. That was all she knew about her.

"Oh. Well, that's cool. I guess. But how are you going to tell your parents?"

"I don't know yet. That's the hard part. It's like,

I don't want them to be mad or hurt or anything. Especially my mother. She might flip."

Anita doesn't need to explain. I can see her mother planted at the front entrance, like a long white, birch tree, wanting to know where Anita was going every time she stepped out. I picture her face crashing down as Anita declares, "Out to find my mother."

"I can help. We can skip like this a couple more times, if it works out."

Anita just shrugs and I decide not to push it. We walk up to Sherbrooke Street and stroll around the McGill University campus. I love the stone buildings, all laid out in a circle. We talk about whether we might end up studying here one day, but it's so far in the future we can't really picture it. My bigger concern is how we're going to get through tomorrow, once we've secured the notes. That's my plan. Anita's father keeps a notepad with his company's name on it beside his office phone. I've glanced in once or twice when he leaves his office for a minute and forgets to shut the door. And my father brings home notepads from the college he works at. They aren't personalized, but they'd be more authentic than plain white paper.

We eat lunch at Harvey's, surrounded by university students, office workers, and some homeless people who are easy to spot because their clothes don't match the season. A few customers donate uneaten fries and cigarettes on their way out and I wonder if Anita and I should do the same. But then

I look down to see that there's not a speck of food left between us. And I doubt Anita would want to part with one of her precious cigarettes.

We decide to kill some time across the street at the Bay. In the furniture department we sit on different sofas and discuss whether they're comfortable enough to buy. The salesman is watching us with hostile eyes and I wonder whether I should ask him to demonstrate how the vibrating bed, which is on display on a raised platform, actually operates. I'd love to see his reaction. Downstairs, we try on heaps of clothes that we have no intention of buying. The salesladies are watching us like hawks because the store is pretty quiet on a weekday afternoon and they're probably wondering what two teenagers are doing here in the middle of a school day. The rest of the customers are old ladies, or younger women with small children in strollers, chomping on tattered stuffed bears.

I take a stack of really neat tops and some jean overalls into the dressing room. I'm just killing time, really. I have no ulterior motives, not here, in a store that I don't really know. But before long that itchy feeling starts to come over me, and I know I just have to take something or I'll die. But I'm kind of scared. I'm out of my league here. I imagine the jail downtown filled with junkies and prostitutes. What if I get caught and thrown in with them. Could I stand it? On the other hand, it would serve my parents right to see me in the midst of such great company.

The whole time I've been thinking these thoughts I've been folding a striped Tommy Hilfiger turtleneck. It's made of nylon and folds up so thin it almost looks like a square of tissue when I'm done. I unhook my bra and lay the shirt flat against my breasts. Then I put my bra back on over it. I can't believe what I'm doing. It's dead out there, there won't be much distraction. I should stop now, but I can't. I'm fueled by the memory of my parents and the way they came back from their last visit with Hannah feeling all hopeful, like things may change. I see myself stomping off to bed and slamming the door, the same way Hannah used to. Finally, I put my sweater back on and look at myself carefully in the mirror. I look bigger, that's all, as if I've just had breast implants.

Anita knows right away and widens her eyes as if to tell me I'm insane. I signal for her to keep quiet and plunk my pile of clothes on the table. Everything now depends on the adults in charge, as usual. The two salesladies are busy gabbing away. One of them peeks at the pile and nods, as if she's content. Lucky for me she doesn't want to miss out on the gossip. The whole time we're descending the escalators and walking out of the store, I feel as though an arrow is about to shoot into my back.

On the way home, Anita and I sit quietly on the bus. The turtleneck itches against my chest. Anita is busy studying her fingers, examining the yellow nicotine stains at their tips. I wonder if she scrutinizes every thirty-year-old woman she sees for signs of similarity. It reminds me of the little bird in my favourite children's book who fell out of his nest and went around asking everything in sight, including an airplane, "Are you my mother?"

I also wonder if, in fifteen years' time, when Hannah is in her early thirties, she'll look at teenagers and wonder if her own child may have looked like them, have listened to the same music and worn the same style of clothes as them, if she hadn't had the abortion.

Chapter 10

I hand my note in to Mr. Curtis first thing, smiling
sweetly to throw him off. It wasn't hard to work up.
My father's signature is easy to find because of the
letters he writes on behalf of political prisoners all
around the world for Amnesty International. The one
I found that he hadn't mailed yet was to help a young
Chinese doctor who had been imprisoned by the
government because he was an AIDS activist and
had been caught at a gay and lesbian film screening.
I can't believe that someone could get arrested for
something like that. There's even a Gay and Lesbian
Student Association at my school, but as far as I can
tell only the president and vice-president, a guy and
a girl, ever show up to meetings. John Fish started
a joke about how these two were really getting it
on in the backroom and just covering up with the
fag stuff. John's always really sophisticated about
these things.

I took the letter into my room and practiced my

father's writing until I had it down pat. Then I took a sheet from his college notepad and wrote that I had had a doctor's appointment at the Montreal Children's Hospital. I didn't specify what the appointment was for because I could just hear my father saying that that was nobody's business but my own anyway.

I felt kind of bad to be using the poor Chinese doctor's misfortune to help save my own skin, but what else could I do? And anyway, the note is gone now, travelling this very minute down the hallway toward the office. It's a bit late for second thoughts.

Anita's note is en route as well. I watched her hand it in, but I haven't had a chance to ask how she managed yet.

At break, I pull her sleeve and hold her back. I can see Jess and Emma and the rest of that gang up ahead. They'll probably want to know all about my new top. The funny thing is that I could barely remember it when I retrieved it from my bra yesterday. I was surprised to find that it was yellow with white stripes and when I tried it on, I realized that I wasn't all that crazy about it. It was as though I'd been in a trance in the dressing room. I steer Anita around the corner and out another door. We end up in the teacher's parking lot, which is, technically, off-limits. Anita immediately lights a cigarette, an added infraction that could get us both suspended.

"Let's hide behind that van," I suggest and we crouch down against the back tire.

"So? How'd it go? Did you get it?"

"Oh, ya, I got it all right." Anita's voice is mean and edgy.

"Well … that's good, isn't it?"

"Ya, it's great. I got grounded for a month. My father caught me in his precious office, just as I was pulling a piece of paper off the pad."

I don't know what to say.

"Oh my God, Anita, I am so sorry. Didn't you wait until he was out?"

"Of course I waited. What do you think I am, a complete idiot? It's just that he knows, he always knows when someone's in his office. It's like he has this sixth sense about it. Once he was cutting the grass, I could hear the machine running, and I popped in to use his phone and he rapped on the window and shouted at me."

"So, what did you say when he caught you? Does he know about yesterday?" If Anita's parents know they might call my parents.

"No, don't worry. I lied. I said I just needed to write a quick note about the music I was practicing and had no paper."

"So, how did you get a note for today? I saw you hand one in."

"Ya, and I'll probably get suspended for that. I did it on a plain piece of paper and I tried to copy my mother's writing from the shopping list. God, Kat, do you know what they'll do to me?"

The bell rings and Anita rubs her cigarette out on the tire of some teacher's van. She holds it there for a while, as if she's hoping it will burn a hole through the rubber.

As we walk back to class, I picture Anita held prisoner in her house for a whole month. She'll probably spend most of it in the dark basement, with just the little light above the piano lit. This punishment is all my fault. It was my idea to skip school yesterday and now Anita is paying. I know the comparison is far-fetched, but I think of the Chinese doctor locked away in his cell when his only crime had been to try to help people.

Just like Anita had been trying to help me.

Chapter 11

I don't change out of my new shirt for Miss Corvette's visit. Let her sit here, with all her connections to troubled teenagers and young offenders, and smile down at me as though I'm the cutest thing on the planet. It would just go to show how dumb she really is not to notice that the shirt is hot, as hot as any of the stuff Hannah has stolen. And, it will be a test to my parents as well. Will it dawn on them that they've never seen the bright yellow turtleneck before?

Miss Corvette is looking a bit more casual tonight. Instead of a skirt and jacket, she's actually wearing corduroy pants and a navy sweater. Perhaps she's gotten to know my parents so well that she no longer feels the need to impress them. They're all buddies now.

I can't figure out why this home visit is necessary. After all, my parents have been having supervised visits with Hannah twice a week for the last three weeks or so. It's not like they need an update.

"Well, Kathleen, how's school going?" Miss Corvette asks, smiling down at me. For a scary second I wonder if my forged note has been discovered after all and this reference to school is the lead in.

"Fine," I respond curtly.

"That's good."

All three adults have their eyes on me.

"Actually, your sister told me that you always did well at school. She told me you're a real brain."

I want to say, *Ya, and did she tell you that she threw her drink in my face because of it*, but I don't say a thing. I don't trust the way this meeting is going.

"Kat's always loved school." My father turns to me, "Right, honey?"

Honey? Sure, I'm a bumblebee in my striped yellow shirt.

"Sweetie, your father is talking to you," my mother now joins in. I can feel her leaning over, tipping the entire sofa in my direction. I'm beginning to feel smothered by all this sudden attention.

"Kat?" my father says, his voice louder this time.

Something inside me snaps. I stand up and blurt out, "What the hell is everyone picking on me for? What's going on here? I thought we were here to talk about your precious Hannah."

The adults are all just looking back and forth at each other. I've never burst like this before.

"Sorry, Kathleen," says Miss Corvette in her controlled voice. "Please, sit back down. Actually, your parents and I did have something we wanted to tell you."

I sit back down, but I don't unfold my arms or look at anyone.

"What we wanted to tell you is that your sister is doing so well and has shown such signs of improvement in her behaviour that she is going to be allowed to come home." Miss Corvette's voice goes high and squeaky at the end of her sentence. "Can you tell us how you feel about this news?"

I don't speak. I feel stung. I wasn't expecting this to happen so soon. I was hoping it never would happen.

"Kat, honey, talk to us." It's my father now. He's using his "I'm your friend and you can tell me anything" voice. This must be his work voice too, the one he uses when he's facing some kid who's just skipped school, or some kid whose eyes are completely glazed over by marijuana.

I still don't speak.

"Well, perhaps it's best if we just leave Kathleen for a while now. She might need time to think. Right, Kathleen?" exclaims Miss Corvette.

I don't even nod. What I'd really like to do is take the heavy tea pot, with steam still rising from the spout, and smash it on Miss Corvette's dyed blonde head.

"If it's okay with your parents, maybe Kathleen can be excused and you and I can deal with paper-work and stuff."

"All right, you can go upstairs if you want, Kat. We'll talk later," my mother says. But I still can't move. It's as though I've turned to stone. It's what I did the night Hannah came home really late and woke me up because she kept smashing into the furniture. I opened my eyes just in time to see her eyeballs spin until all I could see were the whites. Then Hannah collapsed on the floor, between our beds. I knew I should scream for help, but my voice had left me. I was frozen, like I am now.

Then the awful thing was that the next day my sister didn't thank me for keeping quiet about how stoned she'd been. No. The next morning she pulled me right up to her face by taking a fistful of my nightgown. Then she told me I'd better keep my mouth shut if I knew what was good for me.

I know all right. I know what's good for me. But it's never what's good for *me* that seems to count.

Chapter 12

At school the next day, I move from class to class, barely hearing the words my teachers are saying. I drag myself around on automatic pilot and discover that it isn't that hard to do. You can be somewhere physically even when you're elsewhere mentally, as long as you get there on time and stay polite. As long as you open the book to the right page and move your head as though you're following along, no one will notice that you're really far away. Some part of my brain even knows to copy down the homework assignments. I'll be able to do those on automatic pilot as well: answering questions, solving problems, researching the ever-growing hole in the ozone layer that is threatening to burn up the planet. I could do it all in my sleep. After all, I'm really good at school. I'm a real brain, right? Even Hannah thinks so.

At break, Jess and Emma want to know if I've

"bought" anything lately but I just shake my head, even though it isn't true. After I finally left the living room last night I didn't go upstairs like the good little girl I was supposed to be. I snuck out the back door and went right down to the corner store where I "bought" myself a Mars bar and a box of licorice cough-drops. The last item surprised me when I got home. I had no recollection of taking it, yet there it was, safely tucked in the pocket of my jeans. I could vaguely remember smiling at the nice man who ran the store. I'd been careful enough to buy a pack of gum. I could follow my own rules, even when I was only half there.

When I came back, Miss Corvette was just getting into her red sports car. I pulled back into the shadow of some trees on Andy's property to hide. I was afraid that if she saw me she'd rope me into a conversation. It was bad enough that her bright red car was like an advertisement to the whole street that Hannah's case worker was visiting tonight.

If I thought it would reach, I'd have spit on the Corvette as it rolled past into the night.

"Have you ever thought about stealing things for other people, you know, to make some money?" asks Jess, who has strayed away from her crowd to talk to me.

"No, I haven't. You think I'd want to get in trouble for someone else?" I wish that Anita and I had snuck into the teacher's parking lot again. I'm not in the mood for other people. And I've barely had a chance to talk to Anita lately because she has to go straight home after school to begin her punishment for stealing a piece of paper.

"I'd pay you to get me a sweater," Jess continues, like she hasn't heard a word I said. "I could go to the store with you, show you which one I want, and then you could take it later. Seriously, I'd pay you."

I'm only half listening, but the suggestion registers anyway. A way to make money could mean a way to get away from home, now that Hannah's returning. This morning, my parents actually hung around to make sure we all ate breakfast together. Do they think I'm stupid? Do they think I'd believe they just wanted to do something nice for me for no reason, or that they actually missed my company? Instead of staying, I grabbed a piece of toast and left early. I could feel my parents sigh behind me as I slammed the door.

"I'll think about it," I snap at Jess. Then I pull Anita's arm and steer her away, not caring if I'm being rude.

"How are things?" I ask.

Anita shrugs.

"Have you done anything about, you know, finding your mother?"

"Not really. I can't do much from home except surf the net. There are a few Web sites. The trouble is you have to be eighteen to register, or else have written permission from your parents."

"God, that sucks."

"I know. What about you?"

"Well, I found out Hannah is coming back — soon."

"Oh." Anita gives me a sympathetic look. It's so ironic that I'm sad because a family member is returning home, and Anita is sad because she wants to find one. I'd much rather be in her shoes. At least she's the one in control. Things will happen because she wants them to, or not.

Last period, in English class, Mr. Curtis tells me he'd like to speak to me after class. I panic for a second, thinking it's about my fake note. But that was handed in a week ago. I'd have been in trouble before now if it was discovered.

When the bell goes, I sit at my desk and wait. After the class is empty, Mr. Curtis comes over, turns a chair around, and sits facing me, straddling it like a horse.

"So," he says, "how are things?"

Oh God, not another prying adult. Perhaps my parents have called the school and told them everything and now Mr. Curtis has been enlisted to help get me on side.

However, Mr. Curtis doesn't wait for an answer before pulling out a piece of paper. I recognize it as the poem I handed in last week. We had to write a rhyming poem about something we wished for. Thank God Mr. Curtis didn't make me read it to the class.

"I'm curious about your poem, which, by the

way, I thought was very good." Then he proceeds to read it out loud, as if I don't know my own poem.

I wish for the power of a little pill
One that could make me very ill
Ill enough to be sent away
For a very long extended stay
To another land and another home
Where in peace I'd be left to roam
Where I'd be cheerful through and through
And never ever feel blue
Where no one mean could ever hurt me
And those who love me never desert me

I listen to the poem as though someone else wrote it and make sure my face doesn't show any emotion.

"Would you like to explain why you wrote this, Kat?"

"Because we had to," I reply.

Mr. Curtis chuckles. "Good answer. But try again. I mean, what made you express a desire to get sick and go away?" I can feel the way Mr. Curtis is scrutinizing me, his eyes boring into mine, trying to read my mind. I'm not sure if he knows about my situation. Hannah used to be a student at this school, after all. It was here that she was caught breaking into lockers last April. And it was this school she was suspended from. She hadn't returned here, though, for which I am eternally

59

grateful. My parents thought Hannah might do better finishing out the year in a smaller school with an alternative program. And, of course, this year, she was in the group home school.

"Look, Kat, I know something might be up. That story you read to the class got to you, I could see that. And I'm sorry I made you read it. If I'd known there was something painful behind it, I wouldn't have. But, if you do want to talk about it, I'm here, you know. I'd be happy to listen. Sometimes it does good to talk to an adult. If not to me, then maybe to a counsellor. You think about it and let me know, Kat. Okay?"

I nod, thinking how I now have another item to add to my list of things to think about.

But on the way home the only thing I'm thinking about is Jess's offer. Stealing for money.

I figure I probably have nothing to lose.

Chapter 13

Tonight is Hallowe'en. Normally, we carve a pumpkin and hang up some scary decorations, like the six-foot skeleton with paper-clip hinges at its elbows and knees, the big rubber spider, and the door witch. But I just can't imagine we'll do that this year, not with the way things are. My parents and I haven't spoken since I learned about Hannah's return. However, after dinner my father surprises me by hauling out the Hallowe'en box and saying, "Okay. Let's get this show on the road."

I feel silly drawing the face on the pumpkin, with him watching me, as if this is the most important thing the two of us have to work out together. My father and I used to do lots of neat things together. When Hannah and I were little, he took us to protests organized by groups he was involved with, like Greenpeace and Amnesty International, to make us aware of the world, he said. The three of us were chained to a tree on Mount Royal once to protest the mayor's plans to build a revolving restaurant at the summit. Another time, we lit Chinese lanterns and marched with a group through Chinatown to protest the killings in Tiananmen Square. And once we stood with a crowd outside the US embassy shouting "Hell no, we won't go, we won't fight for Texaco," during the Gulf War.

I can feel him wanting to say something to me now, but his mouth is as closed as the mouth of the pumpkin before it gets carved out.

When the pumpkin is done, my father sets it out on the porch, and my mother empties a few bags of goodies into a couple of big bowls. I want to run upstairs and shut myself in my room, but the job of handing out candies has been mine for three years now and leaving just wouldn't feel right.

Slowly, as it darkens outside, the kids come. Most of their costumes are pretty boring. There are a few Batmans and Robins, lots of witches and princesses, and a couple of dogs and cats. Then there are a bunch of Harry Potter and Britney Spears look-alikes. When I was really young my mother would always dress Hannah and me up in matching costumes, like the Scarecrow and Tin Man from *The Wizard of Oz* or two of the *101 Dalmatians*. Once, we were even salt and pepper. She made the disguise out of wire and old sheets. We had holes on our faces for eyes, nose, mouth, but people were supposed to believe that that's where the spices would fall out of the shakers. Salt and pepper, never one without the other.

My parents and I take turns throwing candy into plastic pumpkins and pillowcases. A couple of times, I'm sure I recognize kids from my school. Personally, I think no one older than twelve should be allowed out on Hallowe'en. I hear a tall guy with a voice deeper than my father's call out "Trick or Treat," and I'm sure it's John Fish. His gang would go out. They'll probably hide behind bushes and steal bags off little kids later. I want to call out to my father not to give him anything, but can't. I don't want John to hear me and I'm also, technically, not speaking to my father.

I'm not stupid. I know that tonight's display of Hallowe'en spirit is another one of my parents' ploys to make us seem normal again. To try to cover up the fact that a whole load of fresh lumber is now sitting in the hallway, waiting to be magically turned into a new room for Hannah in the basement.

I'm sure it was Miss Corvette's idea. I can even hear her instruct my parents to give Hannah her own space, to do something that showed they'd put some effort into her return.

Doesn't anyone realize that Hannah was sent away to be punished? I don't get why everyone now needs to bend over backwards to welcome her home. That's what you're supposed to do for heroes, not criminals!

When the last of the candy is gone, at around nine o'clock, my father blows out the candle in the sagging pumpkin and turns off the porch light. I'm glad that Hallowe'en is over. I haven't spent this much time downstairs in ages.

As my parents tidy up, I head for the stairs. But before I've climbed more than three, my father calls me back down to say they want to talk to me. I sigh and grit my teeth. I should've snuck up sooner.

"What?" I snap at them, standing at the bottom of the stairs with my hands on my hips.

"Come and sit down, Sweetie," my mother says, indicating the dining room table.

I pull out a chair abruptly and plunk myself in it without unfolding my arms.

"Kat, we know you're upset. You need to talk to us," my father says.

Rule number 6: get your kids to express their feelings. The manual my father works out of is, after all, similar to Miss Corvette's.

I don't respond.

"Don't you want Hannah to come back? Don't you want us to get back to normal?" my mother asks, trying to open me up.

Normal? Is that what we were before, when Hannah was constantly threatening to kill me, when I'd wake up some mornings to find the limbs of my stuffed animals had been torn off? I realize now that my parents don't know the half of it, since I was always so careful not to tattle on Hannah.

"She's your sister, Kat. You two used to be so close." I can hear my mother's voice catch like it does before she starts to cry. I know I have to escape before that happens.

"Things might get back to the way they used to be if we all try," my father says. "Hannah has been through a lot." He doesn't mention the abortion directly, nobody does. I only found out by eaves-dropping. "You need to be on our side here."

I spring out of my chair and run up the stairs. I don't stop until I'm in my room. There, I pick up Blackie, my oldest stuffed bear. Its left leg is dangling by a thread, the cotton stuffing hanging out. I fling it down the stairs. It lands at the bottom, just a few feet from where my parents are still sitting.

"There!" I yell. "Your precious Hannah did that. Is that the normal you want us all to go back to?" Then I slam my door and shut myself inside my room, the room that is now, deliciously, all mine. I have covered up Hannah's bed with stuffed animals and old toys, with clothes and school work, anything to disguise the fact that it's Hannah's.

Then I sit on my bed and feast on the chocolate bars, candies, and chips that I've been stuffing into my pockets all night long.

Chapter 14

Hanging out with Jess is completely different from hanging out with Anita. For one thing, Jess talks more. She keeps up a running commentary on everything she sees and on every thought she has about everything and everyone. I've never learned so much about the other kids in my class in one afternoon. I'm amazed to discover that John Fish's parents are actually Jess's godparents. According to Jess, he has the nicest parents in the world. She practically makes them sound like saints. Then why is their son such a jerk? How do some kids just turn out rotten, in spite of their families? There must be a gene that programs some kids to get warped. That means it's a waste of effort trying to teach your kids right from wrong. I mean, why bother if they're just going to grow the way they're programmed to, like a tree whose limbs are destined to follow a certain crooked pattern, no matter how well they're pruned?

Jess wasn't kidding when she made the offer to

pay me to steal for her. In fact, she kept bringing it up, until I finally gave in. Now, here we are at the mall on Saturday, going in and out of boutiques trying to find the sweater of Jess's dreams.

"It can't just be anywhere, Jess. Some places are impossible."

"Ya, ya. I know. You told me that already. Don't worry." But Jess keeps leading us into stores where I'd never think of shoplifting — stores with theft detectors as big as bears guarding the door, or stores that are just too quiet and sparse. Finally Jess sees a sweater she wants in a mid-size boutique, one where the clothes aren't plastic tagged. I've worn my loosest sweater and brought a windbreaker too, to put on top. I really want this to work.

I take quite a bit of stuff into the dressing room and tell Jess to hang around. "In case I need a different size, okay?" I say loudly.

I take my time, trying on pants and tops. The only trouble is that the mirror is on the outside of the door. This means I have to go in and out a lot, which gives the saleslady a good look at my size. I try to stay calm and send Jess back to the racks a couple of times for different colours or sizes. Finally, just as I hoped, the saleslady gives up waiting for my decision. That was my plan all along. Confuse, divert, bore. Anything to make the process less neat and ordered. By the time I have Jess's sweater on under my own sweater, with the wind-breaker on top, I'm sweating. I look like I've gained ten pounds in the last twenty minutes, but I can't do much about that now. I heave the pile of clothes I'm not buying onto the counter, thank the woman with my best smile, and walk out, hoping that the ballooning effect of the windbreaker will disguise my new size.

Jess is bubbling beside me, practically jumping up and down, even before we're out of the store.

"Did you get it? Did you get it?" she asks as we step out into the hallway.

I hiss at her to shut up. I focus my eyes on the down escalator. All that matters is getting on it. The metal stairs will pull me down toward safety.

Jess runs down the escalator ahead of me, doing a little dance at the bottom. I want this new alliance to work out, but I also feel like punching Jess in the face. Her energy is going to attract every guard in the mall toward us like a magnet.

"For God's sake," I whisper. "Calm down. You're gonna blow it!" This shuts Jess up and we walk quietly toward the washrooms near the food court. There, I pull off the sweater. I pass it under the stall to Jess and tell her to pull off all the price tags and put it straight into her knapsack. I leave the washroom first. I'd like to keep walking, to distance myself completely from Jess. I don't feel safe with her. I suddenly can't remember why I agreed to shoplift for someone else. Did I really want to impress someone like Jess? What would Anita say if she knew?

Within minutes we're sitting on the bus, heading home. Jess is beaming. She tells me I'm amazing. I try to feel proud, the way I would if I'd just accomplished something really difficult, like acing a math test, but I have to force it.

"Here's the money," Jess says, handing me a ten dollar bill. The sweater actually cost forty bucks, but I can't expect to get full price for it.

I fold the bill into my pocket. I can do the math. It's pretty simple. At this rate, I'd have to steal at least a hundred sweaters to make a substantial amount of money, something that I could use to get away from home. But that could take all year.

And even if I had a thousand dollars, where would I go?

The bus rolls down toward all the familiar landmarks of our neighbourhood, the train tracks, the highway, the orthodox church, and our own school, sitting empty on this Saturday afternoon.

There's nothing to do now but go home.

Chapter 15

My parents are working on the basement room. They've never done anything as major as building a room before. I didn't even know they'd know how. My father has never been the kind of father who runs around the house plugging holes in the roof or plastering walls. He always said people should put their homes into perspective. A home is basically a place for shelter. It didn't have to be perfect. Then he'd compare our living conditions with those of the millions of refugees in the world, most of them living in tents or lean-tos. The house he grew up in, in Saratoga Springs, amazed me when I first saw it. It was enormous, with a tall turret, several bay windows, and a porch that wrapped like a wide belt around the whole house, holding it in. I remember wishing we could live in such a house.

I refuse to go downstairs to see the progress of my sister's new room, but I have taken careful note of all the supplies — pink wall-to-wall carpeting, gallons of paint, a bed and bureau, and even a beanbag chair that I'd love to have myself. They got her a new desk too, which is a total waste of money. As if Hannah is now going to transform into student of the year.

My parents have thrown every spare minute of their time into the room. They're building it in the corner of the L-shaped basement, behind the washer and dryer. I grin when I think how dark and damp that part of the basement is, so damp it's often crawling with pill bugs. No matter how wonderful my parents manage to make Hannah's new room, she'll be tortured every time she walks to it.

Serves her right, when a lean-to or canvas tent pitched in the back yard, well away from the house, is all she deserves.

Miss Corvette even comes over one Sunday, wearing jeans and a sweatshirt, to see the new room, which she has heard so much about.

"What do you think of Hannah's new space, Kat?" Miss Corvette asks me when she comes back upstairs after her inspection.

"I don't think about it at all. As far as I'm concerned, as long as she stays down there, it's fine by me." This gives me a new idea. Perhaps they really are building Hannah her own little prison cell down there, one with a little sink and toilet in the corner. They could install a dumb-waiter to the kitchen and Hannah would never have to come upstairs again. She could be like a pet beast in the basement. Eventually, she'd take to growling and sounding like a caged animal, and we'd be forced to invent wild stories to explain the noise to visitors.

"Your sister is really looking forward to coming home, you know? It may seem kind of romantic, living with a bunch of girls on your own, but it isn't really. It can be very hard. Hannah has found it hard."

I try not to let Miss Corvette's words penetrate the new image I have of my sister's den. Besides, I know all about how hard living with other girls can be. I wonder if Miss Corvette heard about the amputated bear. Perhaps I should go upstairs and bring down the jean shirt that Hannah ripped up the middle. It had been last year's birthday present from my parents. I wore it out to a movie one night with Anita and woke up the next morning to find it cut in half. I never knew why Hannah did it and of course she never confessed. The only thing I could think of was that Hannah hadn't gotten anything that year because her birthday was just after the breaking and entering fiasco. It was my father who held out on that one. My mother wanted to buy her a little something, a token. But my father insisted they'd just be rewarding her bad behaviour.

"Your sister gave me this to give to you. You don't say much, Kat, but I know you're an intelligent girl. Hannah told me so. I know that you won't have any trouble figuring out the symbolism of the gift." And then Miss Corvette leaves. As I watch her red car speed away down the soggy street, I wonder what her real name is. I've heard it before,

72

but I always cancel it out with Miss Corvette, the business woman in the flashy car who speeds in and out of my family's private life.

I open the homemade wrapping paper, which is a collage of comics. Inside, I find a pair of earrings curled up on top of a picture of Garfield. I wait a minute before daring to touch them. They may still be hot from Hannah's hands. Eventually, I pick one earring up and let it dangle. It is at least six inches long and is made of beautiful wooden beads strung together. At the end of each earring a single purple feather is delicately woven into the wire.

They're beautiful. I picture Hannah at a round table with lots of other girls, all of them intent on the afternoon project, something to pass the time since they weren't allowed out. I see her choosing the beads and I wonder what her thoughts would have been as she worked. Did she plan all along to give them to me? Did she think, as she was working, *these are for my little sister*?

Did Hannah worry, as she was stringing the beads together and weaving in the fragile feather, how I would receive them?

Beside the earrings lies a slip of paper. I open it slowly, my heart racing. On it are the words, "Wump earrings. Remember?"

I gasp. The long french fries at McDonalds.

Yes, I do.

Chapter 16

On Monday, Jess wears the new sweater to school. I watch her from across the classroom as she shows it off to Emma. When they turn to look at me, I look away. I made Jess promise not to tell anyone where the sweater came from, but I knew she'd tell Emma. She wouldn't be able to help it.

However, by afternoon, it seems that the whole school knows.

"Hey, there goes the Kat Burglar," John Fish says to his circle of friends as Anita and I walk by, loud enough for me to hear. I feel my whole face flush red. I turn to glare at him, but catch him smiling at me. I try to give him a mean look, but he responds with a wink that disarms me.

"I'm going to kill Jess," I tell Anita. "She's got such a big mouth." John Fish is still following me with his eyes. He winks again.

"Well, what did you expect? God, Kat. You

were really stupid to steal something for Jess. Why'd you do it?"

I shrug. "Well, I've taken stuff for you, haven't I? Remember your music book?"

"Ya, but that's different. That's me. You know I'm not going to tell anyone. But Jess? Since when do you care about her? She's such a show-off."

We wind our way to the teachers' parking lot again, and crouch down behind the same van as last time.

"Oh, well, what do I care if everyone knows? It'll be a whole new business for me. I could expand into CDs and jewelry, no problem. I could become very rich."

Anita rolls her eyes. She doesn't seem to find any of my ideas funny. In fact, she doesn't seem to find anything funny these days. She's become too serious. It's probably this finding-her-mother thing.

"You know, Anita. You should lighten up."

"And you should grow up," Anita snaps back. "Didn't you learn anything from Hannah? Do you want to end up like her?"

I'm so stung by these words, I can't speak. How could Anita compare me to Hannah? I'm nothing at all like Hannah. Hannah did rotten things because she was rotten. She didn't start off bad, I guess. She was the perfect older sister when we were little, always letting me tag along and looking out for me. She just kind of turned bad somewhere along the way. She even started dressing differently one day, in skimpy outfits that had my father shaking his head. He was probably wondering what had happened to the little revolutionary Hannah, the one who had stood beside him in the rain shouting for peace and justice all those years ago, or lit candles at vigils and held them up with such gusto.

Suddenly, I remember something Miss Corvette said at our first family meeting back in April. She had looked at Hannah and asked her what attracted her to troubled people, people who either skipped school or dropped out, people who did drugs and went to bars when they were way underage? What did she feel was missing inside her to make her want to fit in with these people?

At the time, I thought that was all nonsense. It was like Miss Corvette was suggesting there was a big, deep, empty hole in Hannah that she was trying to fill. But the opposite seemed true to me. Hannah wasn't empty. She was full, brimming over with cruel thoughts and gestures. She was more like a volcano than a crater, always ready to erupt and spill her lava over the household.

And now, am I full or empty? Am I changing, the way Hannah did? And why should I even bother trying to figure it out?

"I'll never be like Hannah," I finally spit at Anita, who is finishing her second cigarette. "And you're gonna die of lung cancer before you reach the age of sixteen anyways, so why bother finding your stupid mother?" I snap at her. Then I get up and stamp away across the parking lot. I head to the nearest bathroom, go inside, and lock myself in a cubicle. I sit down on the toilet seat with my pants still on. The whole place smells musty, like rotten pipes. My hands are trembling. I've never fought with Anita before, not in ten years of solid friendship. And what I said to her was so cruel. But Anita had no right to compare me to Hannah. When Hannah was expelled last April, I felt as though a black mark had been stamped on my forehead. I thought the teachers would only know me as Hannah's sister, and that the older kids, especially the ones whose lockers had been broken into, would take their anger out on me. It had happened in April and the rest of that school year was hell. I walked the hallways with my head down, thankful that Hannah and I didn't really look alike.

And yet, it's starting to dawn on me. Though I'd never admit it to Anita, I know I am different. I have changed. There's a whole other side to me now. Did that make me more like Hannah?

The bell rings and I'm grateful to be shaken out of my thoughts. I don't like where they were headed. I look up at the light green door of the stall, and there, etched into the chipped paint with a red marker, is some fresh graffiti.

Want something new?
The Kat Burglar will do it just for you.
Figure this out and you'll know who to find.
She's got the hottest fingers in all of grade
*   nine*

I suck in my breath. I think I may never let it out again. The words have punched the air right out of me. I sit back down on the toilet seat. There is no way I can leave now. I'm a marked person. More marked than ever before. What if this jingle has been scribbled in all the bathrooms, in every stall? What if it's in the boys' bathrooms too? What if Andy sees it?

I can't leave. I won't. And so I don't.

Chapter 17

The next morning, I don't get out of bed. I pull my duvet over my head, blocking out the light. My little cave is dark and hot and I feel the air evaporating with each breath.

Nobody notices that I'm not up and moving about, so I stay in my feather cave, half sleeping, half waking. I'll just let fate determine what happens next. I'm incapable of making any decisions. I'm in the same state as yesterday in the bathroom. After the bell rang, I stayed in the cubicle long enough to wash the graffiti off with wet paper towels. Then I sneaked to my locker, got my coat, and left.

The sharp ring of the phone cuts through my daydream. I have no intention of answering the extension on my beside table. The machine will probably pick up downstairs. I brace myself to hear the message: "You have reached the home of Carl, Louise, Hannah, and Kathleen. We can't come to the phone. Please leave a message." I've been wondering for months why someone doesn't redo the message to reflect the reality of our family, but there isn't much chance of that now.

But the message doesn't come on. Instead, I hear my mother's voice, muffled by all the closed doors between us. A few minutes later she knocks at the door. "Kat! Kat, are you in there?" She opens the door. "Kat, what's the matter? That was your English teacher."

I picture Mr. Curtis asking Anita where I am today. What would Anita have said? "Who knows and who cares?" mostly likely, after yesterday.

"He seems to be concerned about you."

I don't respond.

"Kat, are you sick? Is something wrong?" My mother walks to the bed and sits down. I feel the lid of my feather cave opening up. I don't resist. "What's wrong, honey? Are you feeling sick? Do you have a stomach ache?"

I'm glad my mother has given me an excuse. I decide to just go with it, so I nod my head. But I don't look at her.

"Well, maybe a day in bed will make you feel better then. I'll call him back and say that you're sick, okay?"

I just nod. I feel partly relieved that my mother believes me so easily, but partly annoyed too. She should be able to see that it isn't my stomach that is sore, but my head. She should be able to read my face. But then she hasn't been any good at reading my face in a while. If she could, she would see my new reputation written there — school thief, the Kat Burglar. At your service.

During the day, my mother brings up some tea and toast and later some chicken noodle soup, all her standard home remedies. She leaves them on a tray on my bedside table then vanishes without saying a word.

I watch my mother deliver the nourishment, the food that is supposed to go into my body and make me feel better. I see my mother smile down at me in her distracted way and I think how she has no clue. No clue at all. And it makes me want to scream. I want to scream out at her that I'm bad, that I'm not the good, well-behaved daughter. I'm not who my parents think I am.

And why can't they see it?

Why are they so blind?

I swallow the tea and hot soup, feeling them slide down into my stomach. But they don't fill me up. They only make me feel more empty.

Chapter 18

Next morning, I make sure I get to school early so that I can check the bathrooms before first period. So far, I haven't found any more graffiti. I have to check, though. I have to make sure. I decided yesterday that I can't count on anyone to help me, not even Anita. I have to do things for myself. I'll get rid of the graffiti and just deal with whatever comes up. If my reputation is tarnished, so what? What has a good reputation ever got me?

I'm just stepping out of the bathroom near my homeroom when Mr. Curtis opens the door.

"Ah, Kat," he says. "You're with us today."

I simply nod.

"Are you feeling better?"

I nod again. Mr. Curtis continues to stare at me as if he's waiting for some sort of revelation.

"Remember what we talked about, Kat. I'm here if you need to talk, okay?"

"Thanks," I say. I feel I owe him at least one

word. Something about his caring voice makes me think he knows more than he's letting on. He's probably heard something from Jess. My face reddens. I've been working on accepting that my reputation might be tarnished, but it's hard not to be embarrassed in front of Mr. Curtis.

"I'll see you in a few minutes then," he says. Then he walks off to the boys' bathroom. I can't exactly check in there, can I?

I start off to my locker and run smack into John Fish.

"Hey, Kat. What are you up to? Staking out the place?" John laughs devilishly. Last week he dumped his pencil shavings into the aquarium in the biology lab and screwed up the filtration. I really shouldn't be talking to him.

"Very funny. Ya, I'm thinking up a plan for stealing all the PCs in the lab. Wanna help?"

"Sure, I'll help. But you'll have to give me some tips, cause I hear you're pretty hot, if you know what I mean?" John winks, then he leans very close to me, so close that I can feel the heat off his body. "In fact, I was wondering if you wanted to go out with me this Saturday. You know, we could hang out at the mall, see what's up, that kind of thing." I try not to, but I can't help noticing that John is actually kind of cute. He has great arm muscles, which he loves to show off in short-sleeved T-shirts. He has a perfect body, narrow at the hips and broader across the shoulders, like Brad Pitt. Even their names kind of sound the same — two words, two syllables, with the rhyming "i" sound in the middle.

"Okay, I guess." I can't believe what I'm saying. Am I actually agreeing to go out with John Fish?

"Good, I'll meet you there at one." Then he saunters off, waving back over his shoulder without turning around. I stand there in the empty hallway, watching him. I wonder what it would feel like to be held by John Fish. I imagine him looking at me with his blue eyes and brushing my cheek with his fingers when I tell him how I feel about Hannah. He puts his arms around me more tightly and pulls me in until I am entirely enveloped by him. I feel warm and secure and utterly protected. When he kisses my face, my knees weaken. And when he kisses my lips, my mouth opens wide. I feel the kiss flow all the way down my body, like a rush of energy.

My delicious fantasy is interrupted by the sound of the bell and the doors banging open. I shake my head. I can't believe what I've been thinking about. I need to get a grip.

All day, Anita and I avoid each other. Maybe we're just drifting apart, the way people do. I hang out with Jess and Emma and the rest of that gang. I know I should be mad at Jess, but I don't really care anymore. If Jess wasn't such a bigmouth, John Fish would never have asked me out.

After school, I watch Anita walk off toward her house. Her knapsack is loaded down with books and her shoulders are hunched forward in an effort to keep her balance. She looks as though she's carrying a huge burden. For a minute I think of running to catch up with her, to say I'm sorry, to try to lighten her load, but I don't.

I'm starting to think it doesn't pay to care, to be involved. It's better to be completely separate from other people. That way the things they do can't hurt you.

In my mind, I store Anita in my middle drawer, behind my T-shirts, which is also where I stored the box with the earrings from Hannah.

At home, I'm surprised to see my father home early. He and my mother are sitting at the counter in the kitchen. It's obvious that I've walked into the middle of a serious discussion. You wouldn't have to be Einstein to figure out the topic. I kick off my shoes in the porch and head straight for the stairs.

"Wait, Kat, we want to talk to you."

I sigh. Not again! I step over empty boxes and scraps of lumber, all the leftovers from the basement room project.

"What?" I snap in a tone that tells my parents I don't really have the time.

"Sit down, Kat," my mother says.

My mother wasn't at all surprised this morning by my speedy recovery from whatever was ailing me yesterday. She didn't even ask me about it.

"We found out today when Hannah will be coming home," my father says. "I had to go and have a meeting with Miss Kalputos and Hannah and the woman who runs the group home." It takes me a few seconds to register Miss Kalputos as Miss Corvette. "They seem to think she'll be ready in about two weeks. She'll have finished her term work by then and she can write her exams before leaving."

My father looks at me as though I've been worried about Hannah's ability to finish the school term. Doesn't he know I couldn't care less?

"So?"

"So, we just wanted to tell you. We want you to be part of all this too, Kathleen," my father is explaining. "You live here too, don't you?" I can hear his frustration level mounting.

"So? Good. You told me. Can I go now?"

"Kat." This time it's my mother. "Why are you being like this?"

I can't even begin to answer this question. I shove it away from me, as if it has nothing to do with me. I force myself to think about my date with John Fish instead. I wonder if we'll hold hands around the mall. What if someone from school sees us? The rumour will spread like wildfire.

"… know things haven't been easy." I'm aware only of the tail end of my father's sentence. But I let that trail away too, like the ribboned end of a kite. Finally, my parents wave me away. I'm dismissed. I float up to my room, completely cut off from my surroundings.

Upstairs, I tear through my cupboard to plan what I'll wear to the mall on Saturday, on my date with John Fish.

Chapter 19

Before leaving home to catch the bus to the mall, I take a good look at myself in the full-length mirror, starting at my feet and travelling all the way up. I'm wearing tight black jeans with gold braid down the sides. My top is a tight black T-shirt that barely covers my belly. My dark hair is pulled into a high ponytail, with two loose strands dangling behind my ears to my shoulders. I look like an entirely different person.

I had to take the jeans and top from enemy territory — my sister's side of the closet. Looking through Hannah's clothes was creepy. It was as if her sweaters still held the shape of her arms folded across her chest, and her pants looked full, as if Hannah's limbs were still inside them.

But what could I do? I have no going-out-with-John-Fish clothes of my own. Even the gold hoop earrings are Hannah's.

I put my baggy jean jacket, with its tattered

peace symbols, on top of my sister's clothes, just in case my parents are around. But when I get downstairs I discover they're in the basement room, putting up the finishing touches. They brought home a mirror yesterday and some artsy posters, ones with cheery, smiling people sitting at outdoor cafés in Paris. Their mission is pretty transparent. They're going to try to fool Hannah into being happy by surrounding her with happy images. "Good luck," I mutter as I slam the front door.

Walking to the bus stop, I think how Anita would absolutely die if she saw me. We've always made fun of the fashion girls, preferring a kind of grungy tomboy style of dressing. And now here I am, dressed up exactly like one of the girls we always mocked.

John is waiting between the double doors of the mall, his foot jammed in the door so he can blow the smoke of his cigarette outside.

"Wow, you look great," he says. I smile in response. My heart is racing so fast, I'm afraid he'll notice. I've never officially been out with a guy before.

"Wanna just walk around for a while? Get warmed up?" John says, winking.

"Okay," I reply, smiling up at him.

We stroll around the first floor and John points out stuff in the windows that he either owns or would like to own someday. Outside the Gap, he asks me if I like the new baggy style of khaki pants, with pockets running all up and down the legs. I'm about to tell him I don't when he's distracted by a suede jacket that he swears he's going to own someday. Behind us, a crew of workers is setting up the Santa Claus Village that reappears every year at this time. They're banging brightly coloured boards into the shape of a hut.

At the food court John suggests we stop off for a bite to eat. "I'm a growing guy, you know. I get bigger all the time. I need to keep my strength up," John says, laughing. Everything he says seems to have some double meaning.

I order a slice of vegetarian pizza, piled high with onions, olives, green and red peppers.

"Ooh, you're the healthy kind, I see," John comments. "I prefer high fat content myself. You know, good and greasy. Pimple food, although you can see it doesn't have any effect on me."

My tongue is stopped up inside my mouth, buried under a mouthful of healthy pizza. Even if I wanted to defend myself I couldn't. Why didn't I take a smaller, daintier bite?

"Jess told me your parents are her godparents," I finally say, trying to make some conversation that will help me get to know John better.

"Jess is an idiot," John replies. I don't know if this means that Jess was lying about her godparents, or that they really are her godparents but she's an idiot for other reasons. Either way, that track of conversation's now dead.

I look around the food court. If anyone from school is going to see me and John together, this would be the place to do it. My eyes stop at a gang of guys sitting at the opposite end. I recognize them as John's friends from school. I turn to tell him his friends are here, but just as I look at him he holds up his thumb in a thumbs-up signal. His friends then signal back. The whole exchange makes me a bit nervous.

"Okay. Ready to move on, Kat?" John asks, slamming his empty Coke on the table. He emphasizes my name in a funny way.

As we walk past the various food stands selling hamburgers, fried chicken, and souvlaki, I glance back at the tables to see if John's friends are still there. I scan the thickening crowd, but the only person I recognize is Andy. I'm surprised to see him here. I instinctively pull back. I don't know why, but I don't want him to see me with John Fish. But I'm not fast enough. He looks straight at me, as if my eyes have poked him. Then John tugs my arm and pulls me away.

"You know," he says, as we step onto the up escalator, "I never would've figured you for such a hot babe. You hang around with that funny-looking kid, the fat one."

I feel my blood turn hot. "You mean Anita?"

"Ya, Anita, the one whose number is on all those billboards. As if anyone would call her." John laughs.

I should say something in Anita's defense, maybe something about her incredible talent as a pianist. But the words won't come out.

"And then we all find out that you're Miss Super Cool Shop Lifter. The perfect little Kat Burglar." John puts his arm around me and pulls me close. I'm wedged into his leather chest, exactly where I pictured myself in my daydream.

"I'm one lucky guy, here at the mall with the Steal-to-Order Queen, aren't I?" And then he turns me around and kisses me, right on the mouth. I'm stunned. It's kind of like what I imagined, but not as private, and without the warm feeling my dream kiss gave me. I'm trying to pull back, to get away from his wet tongue that's pushing against my teeth. But the next thing I know, John is dragging me into HMV, the huge music store.

"This is how it's gonna work," he says. "I'll show you which ones I want. And then I'm gonna leave, okay? I'll meet you at the bus stop. There's a bus back at three o'clock. If we time it right, we won't be hanging around. We can jump right on and take off. Just like Bonny and Clyde."

My knees begin to tremble. I've never stolen CDs before. I'm sure they're coded to beep. But John is already halfway down the first aisle. I don't know how to explain that I can't do this. I have no idea what Jess told him, but whatever it is I don't think I'll be able to live up to my new reputation. I look down at the gold braid that runs down the outside seam of my jeans. It suddenly looks cheap and tacky and I wish I could rip it off.

"Are you coming or what?" John has come back to get me. He doesn't wait for an answer, but takes off again. This time I follow. I don't know what else to do. He obviously expected me to just jump into this new challenge. I can't wimp out now. I watch his hand point out three different CDs, all in the Rock section. He wants an Eminem, a Limp Bizkit, and a Marilyn Manson. I feel as though I'm sleep-walking through a nightmare.

"Okay? I'm going now," John says. His tone is suddenly more serious. When he says, "I'll see you at the bus stop," I think I detect an edge of threat in his voice.

I nod okay, hoping my face doesn't show how petrified I feel. This is an entirely different situation. There are no dressing rooms to help me plan and strategize. I feel the vegetarian pizza rotating in my stomach.

I lift the first CD, ignoring my own rule of never looking suspicious. I hold it at arm's length, as if it's contaminated. Then I quickly, too quickly, slip it under my jean jacket, securing it with my left arm. I move to the next one, and the next, doing the same to all three. I have to be careful each time to stack them one on top of the other and to wedge them in such a way that they don't loosen and fall. I'm aware that my arm is too stiff, too clamped down on my jacket. I try to make up for it by swinging my right arm, but it won't move. The thrill that usually rushes through me right about now never happens. I've never been so afraid in my life.

I walk toward the exit which is flanked on either side by tall black pillars. Beyond it the bright lights of the mall shine. Somewhere beyond the mall, John Fish is waiting for me at the bus stop. My feet feel as though they have iron weights in them. I take a last glance over at the cash and freeze. A young salesgirl is watching me. Her eyes widen. She's sending me a signal. She's seen everything. My left arm jerks outward and the three CDs go crashing to the floor. The plastic covers crack and, from the corner of my eye, I see a flurry of movement. Every impulse in my body is imploring me to run, but I'm paralyzed. Then suddenly, as if I'm being propelled forward by an invisible hand, I lurch forward. I fly between the black pillars, down the hall, down the escalator and through the glass doors to the bus stop.

The three o'clock bus is just pulling out. I leap onto it and collapse on the front seat. Way in the back of the bus I see John Fish, sitting with his arms folded across his chest, his legs spread out, taking up the whole aisle. And surrounding him are his friends.

All of them have their eyes on me.

Chapter 20

I flash my bus pass at the driver, who's watching me in his rear-view mirror. I do this automatically, like a robot. The rest of my brain, the conscious part, is still in a deep-freeze. I can hear the crash of the CDs hitting the floor and the ensuing silence. I see myself paralyzed in that position, my left arm jutting out in mid-air. It felt like hours, but it could only have been a few seconds. It wouldn't have taken long for the salesgirl to reach me. Or even for the manager to come running up. The flight from the store, down the escalator and onto this bus, happened in some other time, at some other speed. I was floating and moving in double-time, all at once.

And now here I am, on the bus, with John and his friends waiting behind me. I don't dare turn around. I concentrate on the view outside and work on restoring my breath to its natural rhythm. I'm convinced that some guardian angel was watching over me back there.

"Hey, Kat."

John slides into the double seat beside me, shifting me over with his weight. I continue to stare out the window. I know I won't be able to make my tongue function properly, to make sounds that connect into real words.

"So? Did you get them?" John asks finally.

What does he think? Do I look like someone who's just scored a victory? Does he see any CDs in my hand? What does he think I can do? Make them invisible? Or, does he think they're still nestled snug and secure in my armpit?

I turn and glare at him.

"You didn't get them?" John asks, his eyes widening.

My tongue is still stuck to the roof of my mouth.

John crosses his arms on his chest. "Well, did you get them or not? I thought it'd be easy."

I continue to stare at him. He squirms a bit on his seat. He looks different from the way I remember him before today. I never noticed the light ring of pimples on his chin before.

"God!" he says, when my silent answer finally dawns on him. "I can't believe it. Jess said you were so wonderful. You're not wonderful. You're completely useless. I could've done better myself."

I feel my limbs stir, as though my blood has finally started circulating again, only this time at an accelerated rate. I watch John's face take on an expression of disgust and disappointment. I can hear everything he's going to say about me when he returns to his gang. I hear him spit out the words "useless" and "bitch." But then, he's also going to have to explain why this trip was wasted. He's going to have to tell his friends that their orders didn't materialize. John's the one who's going to look like a failure. This realization gives me strength and I can feel my voice surging back.

"Well, tough shit!" I yell at him. "If you think it's so easy, why don't you take them yourself? Or get one of your goons to do it for you?"

John's face turns red and his whole expression twists, as though he's torn between anger and embarrassment and doesn't know which way to go. Finally, he huffs and stands up. He mutters something back at me, something that sounds like "bloody waste," and then stamps to the back of the bus. With each step I feel as though a weight is being lifted. Outside, the first snow of the year has begun to fall. I watch it descend in a zigzag pattern, blown about by the late November breeze. It makes me think of toboggans, snowmen, and snow angels, all the treasures that snow used to bring when I was younger. I see myself and Andy inside the fort we often built between our houses, with an opening on either side. I see Andy's face back at the food court, watching me and John Fish. He felt betrayed, I could tell. If he were to build a fort now, it would probably be open on his side only.

I would not be invited.

Chapter 21

I stay in my room all day Sunday, listening to my parents bang around in the basement. I lie in bed with a pile of school books beside me and every now and then I pick one up. My eyes run over biology terms and history dates, but not much sinks in. All I can think about is my close call yesterday. I keep seeing the eyes of the salesgirl widening and beaming a message to me. They seemed to scream at me to stop and turn back. If not for those eyes, I'd probably be sitting in some cell right now.

I'm dying to pick up the phone and call Anita and tell her everything. I picture her in her orb of light in the basement, her fingers prancing over the piano keys, producing beautiful sounds. I want to be allowed back in, but I know I'd have to apologize and explain and that requires too much effort right now.

The phone rings several times but I don't answer it. I let my parents do that downstairs, on the new extension they've put in Hannah's room. If the call's for me they never call up to tell me so. The light on my own extension turns red when the line is occupied and a couple of the calls last a long time. It's probably Miss Corvette — or even Hannah, who has called to talk to my parents a couple of times. I feel like I've missed out on a few acts of a play I thought I was attending and can no longer follow the plot. When did everyone but me become so friendly?

At school, the news of my disastrous "date" with John Fish travels around. Even Jess is snubbing me again, as if I've somehow offended her. She even has the nerve to wear the sweater that I stole while walking right past me with her nose up in the air. And, of course, Emma follows Jess. After a few days of this I start hiding in a cubicle in the library at break. That way I don't have to see anyone. At lunch, I watch Jess, Emma, and John from a table way in the corner where I eat my lunch alone. I feel like I'm in quarantine.

Anita sits alone too, at a table way off in the opposite corner. She's wearing a hideous orange sweater that makes her look like a fire hydrant. I recognize the wool. It's the stuff her mother was knitting with the last time I was there.

Only Andy comes anywhere near me.

"Hey, stranger," he opens up, sitting beside me at lunch one day.

"You're not afraid to catch leprosy, sitting with me?" I ask him.

"Nope. In fact, I'm glad to see you away from that gang."

"Oh, really," I say sarcastically.

"Ya, really. Look, I don't know what happened, but I know John can be pretty nasty."

"Well, nothing happened, so don't worry about it."

"But, I do worry about it ... about you, I mean." Andy turns red and stares at his tray. A mound of uneaten spaghetti sits there, along with a bowl of jello and a glass of milk.

"I heard some stuff, I mean I'm sure it's not true, but ..."

"But you thought you'd come over to see if I'm as rotten as everyone says I am. Is that it?"

"Ya ... I mean, no. Not exactly. Look, Kat. We're friends, right? We've been friends for ages. I just want to know if you're all right."

I have no smart response to Andy's concern.

"I was there, you know?" he adds.

"What? Where?"

"At the mall, last weekend. I saw you with John. You were just leaving the food court." Until this moment, I wasn't sure that Andy saw me.

"What were you doing? Following me?"

"No, of course not. I had to get some stuff at the pet shop, for your information." I wonder if he saw what I did at HMV.

"Why, Kat?"

Suddenly, I don't know what he's asking me. Why what? Why did I try to steal some CDs, or why was I at the food court?

"What do you mean, 'why?'"

"Why'd you go out with him? I mean, why would you want to be with someone like *him*?" Andy doesn't say it, but I know he means why someone nasty like John and not someone nice like him. I can't explain it myself.

"And now look what's happening. Everyone's saying you're a kleptomaniac, that John had to stop you from trying to steal everything in the mall. What do you get for going out with him? You get bad-mouthed." Andy pushes his food away as if there's no way he's going to be able to eat now. The spaghetti slides over the edge of the plate onto the tray.

I'm stunned. So that's why I'm the bad guy and John's the hero. That's the lie he's been spreading.

"Is that what you really think of me, Andy?" I stand up.

"Well, yes, no … I mean, I don't know what to think. I don't know you anymore, Kat. Not like I used to." Andy stands up too.

I look at Andy like I'm seeing him for the first time in a long time. I always think of him as a little kid with scraped knees and bangs covering his eyes. But he isn't that anymore. He's tall and kind of cute. He even has a ring of whiskers around his chin.

"I'd like to, though," Andy adds. Then, without looking at me, he picks up his tray of uneaten food and walks off toward the racks in the corner.

This time, I'm the one who follows him with my eyes.

Chapter 22

A huge snowstorm is raging the morning my parents are supposed to pick Hannah up. Out my bedroom window I see a foot of snow piled on the porch roof. The birch and maple trees in the front yard are coated in white. Not even the sparrows have left any claw-prints yet. The front steps look like a baby slide made of solid snow, and the car is a mound of white. At the edge of the driveway, a two-foot ridge of snow has been pushed up by the snowplow that rumbled by minutes ago, shaking the walls of our old house.

Miss Corvette dropped by last night. She was back in formal dress, a three-piece gray suit with perfectly pressed pants. I wondered at first why she'd gone all businesslike again, but then she said she was just coming from a new client's house. I cringed at the word client. Is that what we were? Wasn't a client somebody who voluntarily came to your business? This had been anything but voluntary. I couldn't help wondering about the new family and their circumstances. Was somebody being removed, and if so, was it a child or parent? Were the rest relieved, like me, or distraught, like my parents?

I looked at Miss Corvette's long, perfect red nails and couldn't help thinking of the expression "fresh blood." That's what the new victims would be to her.

Ever since I refused to acknowledge Hannah's gift in any way, Miss Corvette has been treating me more coolly. She doesn't try to draw me in. She doesn't pry to gauge my mental health. She dismisses me, like everyone else does, to some imaginary corner.

"You can come by any time after ten," Miss Corvette said. "She'll be all packed up and ready by then." I waited for her to turn to me and ask if I'd be coming too, but she never did.

My parents didn't have much to say either. They looked at each other from time to time and smiled cautiously. They were either nervous or trying to hide their excitement. I had the feeling that if I weren't there they'd be jumping for joy. I couldn't help remembering the night my parents signed the papers that gave Miss Corvette the right to take Hannah away to the group home five months ago. That night, my mother threw down the pen and ran from the living room and up the stairs crying. But last night she wasn't crying, I can tell you. Not with her darling Hannah coming home.

I waited for my parents to pick up where Miss Corvette had left off, to beg me to come tomorrow, to be part of the family welcoming committee, but they didn't. My father retired to read a stack of documents he was preparing for a seminar and my mother went off to do the dishes.

I simply went up to my room and prayed for a delay.

This morning, the snow has provided it. My parents are now tackling the two-foot ridge. They work diligently, side by side, clearing it away bit by bit, heav-ho'ing, removing the barrier between themselves and Hannah.

An hour later, after they've left, I sit in my room wondering what to do with myself. I can't be here when they come home, I just can't. I'm not ready to face Hannah. I try to remember her face, but the image won't form. The only part of Hannah I see clearly is her mouth, open and angry, shouting at me.

I'm afraid that the minute I see Hannah the air will be sucked out of my body and I'll lose the ability to breathe.

The snow is still falling, steady and persistent. The hedge that separates our property from Andy's is piled high with the powder. If I were still a kid, I'd be outside already, knocking on Andy's door with a shovel.

Well, why not? After all, he kind of made the first move at lunch last week. I tread through the knee-deep snow to Andy's house. I knock on the lion's head, remembering how we used to talk to the brass knocker as if it was real. Andy answers, still in his pyjamas. I didn't even stop to think that not everyone in the world wakes up early Saturday morning to bring home a delinquent child.

"Hi, Kat. To what do I owe this pleasant surprise?" Andy says in his mock grown-up voice, complete with British accent. I can't help laughing.

"Well, I was wondering if you wanted to help me disappear for the day?"

"Oh, yes, jolly good," he answers. "Sporting good fun."

"Andy, shut up. Get serious. Do you want to or not?"

"Ya, ya, okay. Just let me get dressed and gobble something down. I'll be over in a few minutes."

"Great."

I slide back home, pretending my boots are attached to cross-country skis. I don't even bother to take off my coat while waiting. I just kick off my boots and sit at the kitchen counter. The ticking of the clock fills the quiet space around me. If Andy doesn't hurry I might not get out in time.

My eyes are drawn to the basement door. It's odd that there's a room in the house that I've never seen. Before I know it, I'm halfway down the narrow basement stairs. I wish I'd kept my boots on in case of pill bugs. God, those give me the creeps. But, when I get to the bottom, I discover that my parents have installed a dehumidifier and put down some linoleum.

I turn past the laundry room and see the walls of Hannah's new room. My parents have done a much more professional job than I expected. The walls are actually plastered. I turn the door handle slowly, thinking of the myth of Pandora's box and the all the chaos Pandora caused by opening it. I keep my eyes closed until I hear the door bang against the wall. I feel along the wall for a light switch and flick it up. I take a deep breath, count to three, and then open my eyes.

Hannah's new room is beautiful. She has a new bed covered with a pink-and-blue flowered duvet. The curtains are made of matching material. You'd never know that they hide an ugly basement window that's normally covered in spider webs. There's a new pinewood dresser and matching night table. How did my parents sneak these down here without my noticing? And then there's the desk, which I do remember, but it has been transformed. It's now pink with white splotches. The red beanbag chair sits in the corner, waiting to be indented. The walls are covered in yellow-and-blue striped wallpaper that makes the room look taller than it really is, and thick pink carpet covers the entire floor. On a long shelf that runs from end to end along the left wall sit many of Hannah's odds and ends, things that my parents must have taken out of the bedroom upstairs when I was out, things like books, dolls, stuffed animals, trophies, candles, and other knick-knacks.

The sound of the doorbell startles me. Now I

wish Andy had taken longer. I need more time to soak in the details of Hannah's new room. I reach up and take the first thing my fist grabs hold of. It's a brown candle, in the shape of a bear, with the wick sticking out of its head. I vaguely remember it as some birthday gift I myself gave to Hannah years ago. She couldn't have liked it much anyway. She never lit it. I stuff it into my jacket pocket.

I carry a snapshot of the new room up the stairs with me, and then out into the world with Andy. Its prettiness is stamped on my brain, like a bruise.

Chapter 23

"So, where to, Mademoiselle?" Andy asks as we start up the street. The sidewalk plow has just passed, dropping a load of sand onto the path.

I just shrug. I had no destination in mind when I knocked on Andy's door and still don't.

"You choose. I can't make any major decisions right now."

"Well, I guess indoors would be better, right?" My mind wanders to the mall, but I'm definitely not ready to go back there. I imagine my picture posted on "Wanted" signs all over the walls.

"And I guess you don't want to go the mall," Andy says, as if he can read my mind. "That's good. I hate malls anyways. They're a waste of time. Hey, I have an idea. I want to show you where I've been spending a lot of my free time lately. We'll need to take a few buses. Is that okay?"

"Sure. The more buses, the better."

We take a bus up to the northern shore of the island of Montreal, past all the strip malls and fast-food joints that line Boulevard Saint-Jean. The second bus takes us west, way past blocks of apartment complexes and subdivisions, to where the terrain turns more country-like. A few old stone houses hug the banks of the Rivière des Prairies, decorated with wagon wheels, and there's even an antique carriage outside one. Through the trees I watch the river widen into the Lake of Two Mountains, the sun shining on the water's near-frozen surface.

Andy rings the bell and we get off at the next stop. I follow him as he walks into a stand of birch trees.

"Where are we?"

"You'll see. Follow me." He leads the way down a narrow lane. Eventually I see an old house with a sagging wooden porch, set way back amongst the trees. A huge barn, painted bright red, sits to the left of the main house and, on its side, the words *Maison Alouette* are painted in white.

"Voilà," Andy says, holding out his hand.

"Voilà what?"

At that moment an old woman, wearing jeans and a lumber-jacket, steps out of the barn. Her gray hair is pulled up in a ponytail that falls out of the back of an Expos baseball cap.

"Ah, bonjour, Andy. I didn't know you were coming today. You usually come on Sundays."

"Well, I wasn't planning to, Madame Lalonde,

but I wanted to show my friend where I've been working. This is Kat."

"Kat. Oh, mon Dieux. You don't have the right name for this place," Madame Lalonde says, laughing hard. "Well, bienvenue. Go ahead. I will be back soon."

Andy opens the door and I enter the old barn, not knowing what on earth to expect. The first room we pass through has a medicinal smell. Bottles filled with coloured liquids sit on shelves, along with a couple of scales and stacks of rolled-up plaster bandages and towels. Some smaller jars hold cotton balls and swabs. On the opposite counter are lots of wire cages of various sizes, and a stack of old blankets.

Andy then leads me through another door into a room that's bigger than the first and has two huge windows on opposite walls that let in tons of sunlight. The walls are covered in shelves. On each of the shelves sit cages. And in each of the cages are birds. There must be dozens of them, all kinds, black with yellow-and-red tips on their wings, royal blue, cherry red and gold. Some of the birds have little strips of gauze wrapped around their fragile legs or wings. Others are missing a leg and hop around on one foot. None of the birds are flying. Many of them are now squawking or chirping, calling out their hellos, or maybe sending out danger warnings.

"Well, what do you think?" asks Andy. There's a note of pride in his voice, as if what I'm looking at was somehow made by him.

"It's amazing."

"This is what I do," Andy says. "It's my job to set up the cages. Madame Lalonde takes care of the birds. She fixes them up after people bring them here. She's amazing. I've seen her bring birds that looked completely dead back to life. When she has the bird as fixed up as she can it's my job to set up its cage."

I take another look around, studying the cages more closely this time.

"I bet you thought they were all the same. Well, they're not. I try to make each one unique. I use whatever I find lying around — sticks, twigs, stones, leaves, strips of material. I can't prove this scientifically, but I'm pretty sure that having a pleasant surrounding helps the birds get better. I even cut pictures of other birds out and stick them up, like this one." Andy points to one of the higher-up cages. In it is a blue bird with a bandaged wing. On the back wall of the cage is a picture of a bird identical to itself.

"It's a blue jay. A man brought it in last week. He actually witnessed some kids hold it down and cut its wing in half with a pair of scissors."

I wince.

"And this one, the goldfinch. You never see these down where we live — it's too busy — but out here they're really common. This one was trapped in a maze of branches and almost drowned when someone's pond water rose. You see I made her a little pool out of a margarine container, so that she'd get used to being near water again."

I walk around, studying the cages. I feel like I'm touring a museum, looking at works of art. In one cage, Andy has made a kind of teepee structure out of some twigs, tied together at the top with string. Inside the teepee a little sparrow peeks out. In another, a kind of sofa has been fashioned out of strips of flowered material. A red bird is perched like a king on top of it. Some of the rocks that decorate the cages have been painted bright colours, yellow with purple stripes or green with red polka dots. They look like Easter eggs.

I look over at Andy's back. He's busy fussing around inside a cage. It amazes me that he'd come all the way out here every weekend, and that he'd take such care with the cages. His decorations are meticulous and so well thought-out that each and every cage is like a completely different apartment. Madame Lalonde comes back to the barn, carrying a stack of rags. She and Andy huddle in the corner, obviously discussing a bird. I can tell by the way Madame Lalonde is speaking that she's treating Andy like an equal, like someone whose opinion matters. While their backs are turned, I take the bear candle out of my pocket and leave it between two cages. Maybe Andy will find it next weekend and put it to good use.

It's dark by the time we head back. We don't talk much. The birds have left me speechless and I'm tired. I didn't sleep much last night. On the second bus, I put my head on Andy's shoulder and close my eyes. It seems only seconds before he's gently shaking me awake.

"It's our stop," he whispers in my ear.

It takes me a minute to realize what he's saying. Our stop. We're home.

There's nothing to do now but get off the bus and face Hannah.

Chapter 24

I brace myself as I slide my key into the lock, turning it slowly so that no one inside will hear me. I push the door open and stand still, listening for sounds that might tell me where everyone is. But it's completely quiet and the lights are off. When I enter, I find the kitchen light on over the counter, illuminating a piece of paper that reads:

We've gone out for dinner. We waited for you until 5:30 but didn't know when you'd be back. Sorry, honey. We'll see you when we get home. Love, Mom

So, I've missed the homecoming dinner, the celebration meal. Just as well. I wouldn't have been able to swallow anyway, not without choking. I grab some apples, cheese, and juice boxes from the fridge and take them up to my room. I'm not taking any chances. I'm going to hole up for as long as I can.

I turn on the radio and pick up my biology book. My biology exam is first thing Monday morning and it's never been my best subject. I open up to the digestive system and settle in with my apple. But even with the door closed, I still feel exposed. Anyone can just walk in, even though my parents usually knock first. But then I think of Hannah's books and things sitting on her new shelf downstairs. No one asked before coming in to get those. I slide my bureau over a few feet to bar the door. It's exactly what Hannah used to do to keep me out.

Then I settle back on the bed and try to focus on the digestive system. But I still can't. Now that I'm secure in my fortress, there's only one thought on my mind. Andy walked me to the door, just like a guy in an old-fashioned movie. Then he took off his glove and ran his finger over my cold cheek. Apple cheeks, he called me. Then he leaned down and kissed me. I could feel the steam rising where Andy's warm lips met mine. It was the kind of kiss I had imagined, one that made time slow down and the world melt away. It was a kiss that made me tingle all the way down to my toes.

I hadn't told Andy that today was the day of Hannah's return. But he seemed to know. I could tell by the way he said "Good luck" before leaving.

And now here I am, locked up against Hannah's return in an empty house. I locked myself up like this the day Hannah left too. Only at the very last minute, after I had heard the front door close, did I part the curtains to peek out. I was just in time to see Hannah bending into the red sports car. If you didn't know the circumstances, you'd just think Hannah was lucky to be going for a ride in a Corvette.

My family could've waited a bit longer for me to get home before going out for dinner, although really I'm glad they didn't. Now, this space is mine and mine alone. No one is here to cut into my thoughts.

I put my biology book down and close my eyes, drifting off with an image of Andy in my mind. It seems hours later when I hear noises float up from downstairs. I recognize the sounds — boots being kicked off, hangers scraping, the clunk of the kettle. And, finally, footsteps on the stairs. I hold still and try to identify them: are they heavy enough to be my father's, are they medium ones that could belong to my mother, or even lighter than that — the footsteps of Hannah? I feel like Goldilocks, about to be discovered by the three bears. I hear a voice, someone is saying my name. It's my mother. I don't shift or answer. They know I'm home by my boots and jacket, but that doesn't mean I have to participate. I have every right to stay put. I suddenly remember my father, my sister, and me chained to the tree on Mount Royal, standing our ground, staking our claim against the men with the chainsaws. This is the same. I will not let myself be invaded.

I will not help Hannah cut me down again. Eventually, my mom goes away.

Chapter 25

I awaken before the sun is up. More snow has fallen overnight, covering the house and yard in a thick shroud of white. The plough hasn't even gone by yet. It's a perfectly dead Sunday morning.

I'm famished. My stomach is churning. I get out of bed as quietly as I can and slip my cold feet into my teddy bear slippers. I'll just sneak down and get more food. If I bring enough up, I can just spend the day in bed studying.

I pad down the stairs, trying to avoid the creaky spots. The only sound is the humming of the fridge. I pull the handle gently, trying to minimize the clicking sound that it usually makes. I take out more portable food, the same as last night, and I also grab a box of chocolate chip cookies from the cupboard. There's certainly enough food here to keep me from starving for the day.

The rubber tray that holds our slushy winter boots sits beside the kitchen door. I can't help noticing Hannah's boots, or at least they must be Hannah's. I've never seen them before. They're black leather ankle boots, with lace up strings and thick soles, the type that are meant to grip the ice. I wonder where Hannah got them? Did the woman who ran the group home shop for the girls? Did she take them shopping in a group, all of the girls holding on to a string, like nursery school kids? Or had my mother been buying Hannah things and sending them to her through Miss Corvette?

I peek into the closet beside the front door. Sure enough, a new jacket is hanging there. It's a gray ski jacket, the overstuffed kind I like, with lines of stitching wrapping horizontally around to make puffs.

Who would have thought that getting locked up in a group home could get you a whole new wardrobe?

Just as I'm thinking this, I hear some movement on the basement stairs. Hannah and I used to try to scare each other with stories about mice and rats invading the basement at night. But these can't be the footsteps of rodents. They're too heavy.

It must be Hannah.

I'm partway down the hall when the basement door starts to open. I wish I hadn't forgotten to turn off the kitchen light. It illuminates the entire hallway, right up to the door Hannah is now open-ing. I freeze. The door seems to be creaking open in slow motion, the way a door in a horror movie does when the evil guy is lurking behind it.

I find a way to make my legs carry me to the bottom of the stairwell that leads upstairs. I lean back against the wall, hoping the darkness of the stairwell will hide me.

Hannah stands in the doorway, trapped in the light of the kitchen, her eyes, which aren't yet accustomed to the brightness, squinting. I don't make a sound. I stand there, trying not to breathe, looking straight at my sister. Hannah's hair, which was almost down to her waist when she went away, is so short it looks as though she's been shaved. It sticks out all over her head in one-inch spikes, like a convict's.

Hannah looks around as though she's trying to remember where she is. Or as though she's trying to determine if it's safe to come out. Hannah's never done this before. She normally stamped around wherever she wanted, slamming doors behind her.

It wasn't like Hannah to be mousy.

Then, as if it has suddenly dawned on Hannah where she is, she retreats into the basement doorway and pushes the door closed, shutting it softly behind her.

I listen to Hannah's footsteps returning to the basement. I picture her feeling her way in the dark to the laundry room and, behind it, to her cage.

Chapter 26

I try to study for my exams all morning. English will be a breeze. It's my best subject. But Biology is going to be hell. I've been trying to memorize the inner workings of the human body, the components of human blood, the makeup of cells, but nothing seems to stick. By noon, all the food I snuck up early this morning is gone and my stomach is grinding with hunger.

I have two options — starve, or risk seeing Hannah again. I can't get the picture of Hannah, caught like a frightened animal in the glare of a headlight, out of my mind. I try to visualize the digestive, respiratory, cardiovascular, and nervous systems. But I can't. The image of Hannah keeps superimposing itself over them.

I picture Hannah hollowed out, her insides replaced by removable organs, like the plastic body at school. My biology teacher disassembles the various systems, then calls on a student to snap the organs together, like a puzzle. I see the plastic parts of the last system, the one I haven't begun to study in detail yet — the reproductive system. Hannah's has already been used, at the age of seventeen. A teeny-tiny embryo began to form in my sister's uterus. The egg, or ovum to be technical, travelled down the fallopian tube where it met with a tadpole-like sperm. And then my niece or nephew began to grow.

The question is, whose sperm was it? I have no idea how many weeks or months along Hannah was when she had her abortion. I only know that it happened shortly after she went to the group home. Miss Corvette took her. My parents weren't even given that option. That was the law. They didn't even need to know that she was pregnant. But Miss Corvette had told them anyway, a couple of weeks after Hannah left home. That was one meeting I was not called down to attend.

I push my bureau away from the door. No one has tried to talk to me since my mother came up last night. No one has knocked on the door and said, "Kat, come out and say hello to your sister" like I thought they would. And Hannah hasn't come upstairs to bang on the door either, demanding to get in and take the rest of her stuff.

I tiptoe down the stairs, my ears sharp, poised to take in any sound that might tell me what's happening. I should've looked out my window to see if the car was there. Maybe the whole family has gone on an outing, up to Mount Royal perhaps, to the look-off, where you can see far across the St. Lawrence River to the foothills of the Adirondacks in the United States. Would they really just go off and not even invite me?

I would've refused anyway, but the idea that my family has left without me makes me mad enough to forget about being quiet. I stamp down the rest of the stairs and storm into the kitchen.

Hannah's hand jerks on the frying pan handle as she lets out a frightened gasp. The fried eggs, which have just been cracked open and are still watery, slide over the edge of the frying pan and dip into the gas flame.

I freeze. Hannah is standing less than three feet away. She isn't dressed yet either. We're in matching flannel nightgowns — red with teddy bears — Christmas presents from our mother almost a year ago.

We stare at each other. Hannah is still holding the frying pan in midair.

"Hi, Kat," Hannah finally says, in a small voice.

I don't respond. I'm too stunned. I didn't notice this morning how skinny Hannah has become. Her collarbones stick out like two sharp bulbs below her neck.

"Mom and Dad went out to get groceries."

Mom and Dad? Since when did Hannah refer to our parents as Mom and Dad? God, has she been watching reruns of *The Brady Bunch* for the last five months?

Hannah's eyes look enlarged in their big, bony sockets. The eight holes in her ears are empty.

"Do you want some fried eggs?" Hannah asks, tipping the frying pan toward me. "I can make them pretty good now."

I don't believe that Hannah isn't setting a trap and that just when I say yes she won't hurl the eggs at me. In my mind, I hear her say, "Do you want it? Do you really want it? Well, here!" Then I see her throw the jam jar full force, and it glances off my chin. That bruise lasted a whole month.

I know I have to block Hannah out or things will spin out of control. I'll be eating Hannah's food and listening to her lies. I'll be pulled into her vortex, helplessly pinned down. I walk past Hannah to the fridge, yank it open and pull out some more portable food. Then, without looking at her, I leave and go back up to my room. I sit on my bed and gorge until my stomach turns into a heavy rock. Then I get dressed. I can't be in the house alone with Hannah, not now that I've seen her. There was a look in Hannah's eyes that I have to get away from. A look that shouldn't be there. A pleading look. It would have been easier to deal with the old look, the one that cut me down sharply. That was a look that pushed me away. This look threatened to draw me in.

I throw my coat and boots on and slam the door. At Andy's house, I knock on the lion's head. No one answers for a long time. I'm about to give up when Andy finally appears.

"Hey, Kat, what's up?"

"Can we go back to the bird hospital?" I ask breathlessly, barely waiting for Andy to finish speaking.

"Today? I can't today. Jeff and I are studying for the biology test." I look over Andy's shoulder at Jeff who is smiling down at me.

"Oh, thanks a lot," I snap. I fly down the stairs, leaving the two guys looking confused.

I trudge through the snow and slush. God, I hate slush. It's like walking through thick, lumpy soup. I forgot to grab some gloves and my fingers are throbbing with cold. Every second house I pass is in the process of being decorated for Christmas. At one, a man is up on a ladder stringing lights, his two kids steadying its base below him. Further on a woman is hanging a wreath and wrapping pine boughs around her door frame. Each scene looks just like the front of some sucky Christmas card.

Anita's mother answers the door. "Oh, Kathleen," she says, as though she never expected to see me again.

"Hello. Is Anita in?" I'm fighting hard to stay polite. What I'd really like to do is push the old witch down and use her as a doormat.

"Yes, she is. Come in, I guess." I kick off my wet boots then stoop down to straighten them on the rubber mat. The ritual is stamped on my brain.

"She's in the ..." Anita's mother starts to say.

"Ya, I know where she is. She's always in the

basement." Anita's mother holds her breath, and her body seems to grow even taller. I suppose I should apologize, but I can't. I'm not sorry. I'm not sorry at all.

Anita is practicing her scales. Up and down and up and down, like a machine. She doesn't hear me coming.

I tap her on the shoulder and she jumps.

"Oh my God, you scared me to death," Anita says. "What are you doing here?"

"I … I just really felt like seeing you. It's been ages. I …" I'm at a loss for words. I don't know how to explain or where to start. "Look, let's get out of here. Do you want to? We could go somewhere."

"I'm supposed to study."

It's just my luck that on this particular day everyone on the planet has decided to turn into a goody two-shoes. I bet John Fish isn't studying. Maybe he'd take me back to the mall. He could give me another chance. With my mood the way it is, I could steal anything, anything at all.

"Look, it's your last chance. Do you want to come or not?" I suddenly know exactly where I want to go. And I'll go on my own if I have to. I turn and Anita follows me upstairs.

Anita's mother is sitting on her perch. I can tell she hasn't forgiven me for being fresh. She gives me a piercing look.

I swear she can see what I am planning to do, plain as the nose on my face.

Chapter 27

The way I see it, I have three choices. The first is to go back home and become Hannah's little sister. I could find a way to look up to her again, like I did when we were little. I could follow her around and eat her fried eggs. The second choice is to go back home and fight Hannah all the way, to refuse to give up my newfound space. It had always been right down the middle with the two of us, at first. The bedroom, the cupboard, an apple, a pack of new crayons — all shared fifty-fifty. But by the time Hannah went away it had changed to more like eighty-twenty, with Hannah controlling the lion's share.

The third choice is to become someone else altogether, to change from Kat, little sister of Hannah, to New Kat. Hannah would not even be a factor in my new life because it would have nothing to do with her or anyone else in my family. My importance would lie beyond the four walls of that stupid home that Hannah's now invading.

The bus rolls up to the mall and lets out a big sigh. I suck in my breath. I haven't been here since the HMV fiasco. But that was Old Kat. In grade two our teacher made the class paint a giant banner that said, "Today is the first day of the rest of your life." It didn't make any sense when I was seven. But now I understand it completely.

The mall is quiet today. That's because the stores only open at noon on Sundays. Even though I'm now New Kat, I don't have the nerve to go up to the second floor of the mall, where it happened. Not that anyone would recognize me. I was wearing completely different clothes that day. Today, I'm in old frayed jeans and my bummy ski jacket. My hair is down and unbrushed and I'm not wearing any jewelry or makeup. And I'm not with John Fish. I'm with my old sidekick, Anita. Good old, solid Anita. I'll have to include Anita in my new life. There's something so stable and unobtrusive about her. She isn't somebody who takes up all the space and attention. She stays on her side of the line — fifty-fifty.

"Are you sure you want to be here?" asks Anita.

"Ya, of course. Why wouldn't I?" I say in my most lighthearted voice. I'm not sure what Anita knows about my "date" with John. "Let's get some fries. I'm starving."

Even the food court is quiet today. The food stalls are decorated with tinsel and candy canes, even the ones that technically don't have much to do with Christmas, like the Beijing Wok and the Tel Aviv Falafel. Tinny Christmas songs fill the air, trying to get everyone in the mood to shop. Every now and then the mall Santa lets out a big ho-ho-ho. Some kid is probably sitting on his lap, trying to pull off his beard.

"Let's go to the Bay," I suggest next. "I want to look at jewelry for Christmas presents." I'm amazed by how easily New Kat can lie, even to her best friend. Who would I be buying Christmas presents for?

We pass Santa's village on the way to the Bay. A long lineup of kids has formed, all of them eager to share their wish list with Santa. A huge toy train stacked with wrapped boxes runs around and around on a track set down in fake snow. It seems like centuries ago that I waited to see Santa myself. I feel like yelling at the kids to forget it and go home. It's all fake. There's no such thing as Santa, the beard is cotton, your parents buy your presents and fill up the stocking. There's no way some big fat guy could get down a chimney anyway.

In the jewelry department Anita and I twirl the racks that sit on glass counters where outlines of snow angels have been sprayed onto the underside. The poor saleslady is wearing a red Santa cap. I wonder if she did this voluntarily or if she was ordered her to. I point it out to Anita and we chuckle into our sleeves.

I can't believe how easy it is to slip a pair of gold hoops off the rack and into my pocket. I've never stolen jewelry before, but now I can't understand why not. It's a thousand times easier than clothes. I spread out the earrings that are left to cover the bare spot. If Anita knows what I'm doing she doesn't let on. I take two more pairs, some hearts and some pearls, the exact same way, but from different carousels. The Santa saleslady doesn't seem to notice. She seems to be half hiding behind her cash register, looking the other way. She's probably embarrassed about the hat.

We leave the jewelry department and travel over to the hat, glove, and wallet section of the store. I've always wanted a pair of leather gloves. I find a pair I like, lined with rabbit fur, and slip it into my jacket pocket. This Anita does see. I can tell by the look she gives me. It's an exasperated "Are you crazy?" kind of look. Tough. If Anita doesn't like the new Kat, then she can just step out of her life.

"I think we should leave now," Anita says, emphasizing the word "leave," as though she's warning me about some incoming danger, like a typhoon.

"Why? We just got here. Relax, will you? You worry too much." I'm aware that this is how our last fight started, but I can't stop myself. I'm so buoyed up with confidence that I could keep going all afternoon.

"I mean, if you want something you have to

take it, right? Or make it happen. Like, that's what you should do too, Anita. Don't wait for your parents to give you permission to find your real mother. She's your mother. You should just go out there and do what you have to do. If your other mother gets hurt, tough. That's just life, isn't it? Sometimes people get hurt. "

I know that I've said too much, but I continue anyway. "Your mother doesn't deserve you, you know? You're too good for her. What has she ever done for you? She's screwed you up, that's all. That's why you smoke so much. You should just drop her, her and your father. Let him have his precious office. You're way too good for both of them."

Anita's face is completely flushed now.

"You should find your new mother and move in with her. Start a whole new life. Your mother and father won't be able to do a thing. It's your life."

By the time I finish my speech, I've stuffed a leather wallet into my other coat pocket.

"You're crazy Kat, you know that? I may smoke too much, but you steal too much. Way too much. At least I know why I smoke. Do you know why you steal?" Anita's careful to whisper, but it's a harsh whisper, one that still manages to convey her anger. Then she spins on her boots and starts to walk away. "I'm going home to study."

I'm totally surprised that Anita has the nerve to leave. But then I remember that I'm a new person as of today, one who doesn't really care. I shrug.

129

Let her leave. Who needs her anyway? I'm totally in control. And I don't need to know why I steal. Who cares? I do it because I can, because I'm good at it. That's all I need to know.

When I can't see Anita anymore, I take the escalator up to the second floor of the store where a pink angora sweater catches my eye. It's so soft, I can't stop running my hand over it. I love it. It costs $90.00. There's no way I'd ever be able to buy it. I take it into the dressing room. I know this is reckless because I have nothing else with me to return, but I keep it on under my old sweatshirt anyway. If there's a hidden camera, I can't see it. Besides, I stole the turtleneck from the Bay downtown, no problem.

I can't believe it worked. This day is turning out so well. There isn't a hesitant bone in my body, yet some part of me knows that it's time to leave. I have too much on me. I can't even remember what, apart from the sweater.

I descend on the escalator to the first floor of the store and head toward the exit to the mall. I'll catch the bus and go home. I'm not worried about going home now. It has nothing to do with me. I'm removed.

As I step out of the store, a hand grips my arm. I turn to see a woman in a long tweed coat. She's carrying a Bay shopping bag that's bursting full. She must have mistaken me for someone else. I try to shake her arm loose, but she just holds tighter. It's odd that she's wearing open-toed shoes. Her boots must be in her shopping bag. Maybe she's some kind of escaped lunatic. I open my mouth to tell her off, but she cuts in.

"Store security, Miss. You'll have to come with me."

Chapter 28

Within seconds, another woman appears. She's wearing navy pants and a blue shirt. On her sleeve is a yellow badge that says *Security*. The two women take hold of my arms and walk me, as if I'm an invalid, through the store. I'm only vaguely aware that all the people we pass are turning to stare. I hang my head down, tucking my chin into my collar the way criminals do when they're captured by a TV camera. The walk is happening in slow motion, the way a bad accident does. Like the fall I took last year on the stairs. Hannah had been pushing me around on the upstairs landing. I can't even remember why. The next thing I knew I was tumbling down. It could only have taken seconds to reach the bottom, but while it was happening time slowed down, and it seemed to take forever to roll from step to step. I even had time to think how glad I was that the stairs weren't still bare wood. My parents had carpeted them the previous year when my grandmother had come to visit, in case she fell. I was thinking that because the stairs were carpeted, the bruises wouldn't be too hard to hide from my parents.

I snap back from my daydream to discover that we've taken the up escalator and are now walking through the appliance section. Even the tall white fridges seem to be staring at me, as do the stoves, each of their burners like a black eye. When we pass the wall of television sets, I expect to see my own face projected there. Breaking news. The Kat Burglar has been caught.

By the time the two women usher me into a small office at the back of the store, my knees are trembling. We're met by the store security manager who takes over, dismissing the security guard. The store detective, the one in the disguise, stays. The manager lifts my arms straight at the sides and pulls the stolen goods out of my pockets. I feel like I'm watching a magic show. He's pulling ribbons out of sleeves and rabbits out of hats. By the time he's finished, there's a heap of stuff on the desktop. Three pairs of earrings, leather gloves, and one leather wallet. He ends his act by pulling out a silk scarf that I only vaguely recognize. I feel like I'm being stripped. I'm raw and naked, fully exposed. I can't believe I took all these things. I want to shout that they've made a mistake. It wasn't me. It was someone else, someone who's trying to frame me, someone who wants to hurt me. But a tiny voice in my head, one that sounds like a scared animal, whispers to me that I've done this to myself.

Then the manager ushers me into a metal chair. He points to the stash and begins pumping me with questions. My name, my address, my phone number, my age. I don't resist. I tell him everything, retrieving the information like a computer from some still-functioning part of my brain. But when the questions get more complicated, I drift away. I can't focus. From time to time I hear words like "parents" and "police." They prick my brain like needles, shocking me back to the moment, but then I slip away again.

When the manager gets nowhere, the store detective has a go. She speaks more softly. She wants to know what I think my mother is going to say. All I can do is stare at the woman's feet. The shoes are all wrong. I can see that now. They're a dead giveaway. She should be in boots. Everyone is in boots now. Her toes would freeze off in open-toed shoes in this weather.

I remain silent. My mouth has stopped working. I'm not trying to be cagey, I just can't open my lips. I can't produce any sounds. I have no words to offer. No explanations. In my mind I see Anita walk away. I hear her ask why I steal. It's the same question the lady detective is asking me. Why did I do it? Do I know how much trouble I'm in? Do I know I might have a record now? Do I know … do I know …?

I know nothing. I hear the manager say he's going to have to call. I don't know who he'll call. My parents or the police? And what does it matter? One is just as bad as the other. The police will treat me like a criminal and try to scare me. My parents will look at me like I'm some kind of stranger. Their good little daughter, the honour roll daughter. The one who can look after herself without any supervision. The easy, no-maintenance, wash 'n' wear daughter.

Let them come. Let them see how little attention I really need. Let them see what Hannah has done to me.

I'm finally left alone in the office. It's a bare white room, not a single picture or poster on the walls. The only pieces of furniture are a desk and two metal chairs. The whole thing looks fake. It's a fake office that they just pretend to use. But really it's where they try to break down people like me, people who've done something wrong. It's bare and white and cold, so people will be uncomfortable and say anything to get out of here, confess to anything. Perhaps there's even a two-way mirror somewhere. They have left me alone so that I can take off the angora sweater. Maybe they're waiting to see me strip, their eyes plastered to tiny holes in the wall. It'll be like a peep show for them. The manager will get his kicks for the day, seeing me in my bra.

I huddle under my ski jacket while I take off the two sweaters. I lay the stolen one on the desktop beside the rest of the items and quickly put my sweater back on. I'm cold. The skin on my chest and arms is goose pimpled.

Suddenly, I think how if Andy were here, he could turn this cold room into a comforting cage. He'd hang up some pleasing pictures for a start. He'd replace the hard folding chairs with cushioned ones. He might put a pile of straw in the corner for me to curl up in. And he'd put one of those round rice paper shades in a soft colour, like tangerine or turquoise, over the bare bulb. Anything to cover up this stark white glare that I'm caught in.

I sit alone for over an hour. I can't believe I'm in the same mall that I used to love. I can't remember what I loved about it. Its brightness and shininess just seem cold now. And, if I ever get out of here, I never want to look into any of those metallic mirrors again.

The lady detective brings me an orange juice and a packet of Dad's cookies at some point, then leaves again, probably to catch more shoplifters.

Eventually, just when I'm starting to think that the manager has gone home and forgotten me, he returns. He announces in a loud voice that they've found someone to take me home.

"I want you to know that you're very lucky. Because of your age, and because we have been assured that you've never done anything like this before — the police have no record on you — we're going to let you go with a warning. However, young lady, if you ever think of stealing anything, even a stick of candy, from this store again, you will have to deal with the police and the juvenile authorities.

So don't be foolish again." He pauses and stares down at me, as if he's waiting for a reaction.

"Don't choose the wrong path, Kathleen. It's not worth it, believe me." His voice softens at the end of his speech, and he lays a hand on my shoulder, almost in a fatherly way. I can't look at him. The pressure of his fingers on my shoulder is threatening to open me up, to crumble me under their weight. I hold myself tight. I won't cry now.

The manager opens the door and motions for me to leave. I step out of the office and look up. I'm expecting my parents to be standing there. I'm braced for their look of disappointment. I know that look well, that hopeless look that cried out for an explanation. I've seen it often enough when Hannah did something outrageous, something for which there could be no logical explanation.

But when I look up it's Hannah's face I see, gobbling me up with her huge eyes.

Chapter 29

Neither of us speaks. I study the tiled floor beneath my feet. I don't know what to do. Why is Hannah here? Did my parents send her, in order to force me to confront her? I'd rather go back into the white room than deal with her.

Hannah eventually turns and walks away. I follow. What choice do I have? We leave the store and the mall in complete silence. When we're settled on the bus, Hannah finally speaks.

"You're lucky Mom and Dad weren't home when they called. I asked if I could take a message, and when they said it was store security at the Bay, I figured it out. Then I lied and told them our parents were away for a week and that I was in charge of you. I told them I was eighteen. It's just a little white lie."

I try to calculate Hannah's age, but can't. I line the numbers up but they keep slipping. I look out the window, watching as the bus rolls through the slush, spraying innocent bystanders. When they shake their fists up at the taillights I imagine they're actually expressing their anger at me.

"You're lucky I've been around the block, Kat. Not everyone would've known that you were in trouble right away. You'll thank me for this some day." Even if I did want to thank her, which I don't, I couldn't because my voice is still plugged up.

"I've heard the way authority figures speak often enough. They have a certain expression in their voices, like everything is a matter of life and death. I would've known who they were even if they hadn't said," Hannah continues.

I can't believe she's actually bragging about the fact that she's gotten into trouble so many times. The way I feel now I just want to bury my head in a snowbank, like an ostrich in the sand.

A few blocks later, Hannah reaches up and pulls the bell. We're only halfway home. "Come on. We're getting off here," she says firmly. Then she grabs my arm and practically pulls me off the bus.

Hannah leads us around the block to a park. I can't believe I'm already following her around like a stray dog. She plunks herself down on a bench and wraps her arms around her chest. Her puffy ski jacket swallows up her thin body. I sit down too, but on the opposite corner of the bench, well away from her.

"Okay, Kat. What the hell were you thinking?"

Hannah asks firmly. A huge lump gathers in my throat.

"Come on. I'm waiting." Hannah stands and places herself right in front of me. She's tapping her black boot on the ground. I wouldn't be surprised if it flew up and kicked me in the face. I have to defend myself fast, or I'll be lost.

"It's none of your business. Who do you think you are all of a sudden. My mother?"

But Hannah is undeterred. "I mean it, Kat. I want to know what you were thinking back there. I don't care what you think of me. I really don't care at all. You can be as angry with me as you want, but I want to know what you were doing. Do you have any idea what this will do to Mom and Dad when they find out?"

I gasp. Hannah caring about our parents! Maybe she had a lobotomy while she was locked up. On the other hand, it would be just like her to run home and blab. She can't wait to get me in trouble. She won't keep her mouth shut like I did all those times.

"Since when do you care about them and what right do you have to be telling me I might hurt them? Ha! That's a good one. You've already completely ruined their lives." I expect Hannah to looked crushed when I blurt that last bit out, but she looks totally unshaken.

"I know what I've done to them, Kat. You don't need to tell me. I've had plenty of time to think about all that. What d'ya think I was doing in that hellhole for all these months? Weaving baskets?"

"Oh, well, isn't that just swell. So you know what you did and now everything's fine! I'm so relieved. Now we can go home and be a big happy family again. Isn't that cozy?"

"Kat, grow up, will you? Nobody said anything about happy and cozy."

"That's right. No one said it, and it's never going to happen. Do you even know that Mom and Dad and I hardly even speak to each other any more, all because of you? Just because you had to be so stupid and selfish all your life. You're like a tornado, blowing everything in your path down. I don't want to have anything to do with you ever again. So drop dead! It's none of your goddamned business if I want to shoplift. I'll do whatever I want. If I want to, I'll go back to the mall tomorrow and steal some more, and you can't stop me!" I'm practically screaming now.

"Look who's a tornado now! Nobody can stop you? Well, I'm going to try, if I can."

"Oh, ya! And why is that?"

Just then a squirrel scurries down a maple tree near the bench. It stops dead at the bottom and freezes when Hannah sits back down.

"Because, Kat," Hannah's voice goes soft and she looks down at the ground, "I know I hurt you too. I spent a lot of time thinking about that as well."

I don't know what to say. This could be a trap. It could be Hannah trying to get some sympathy.

She's done that before, and then just when I think she's changed, bam! Hannah would shove me hard against the wall for stepping on her side of the room.

"I want to tell you something, Kat," Hannah says. She takes a deep breath and continues: "When they took me away I didn't care at first. I was getting away from home, which is what I thought I wanted. I wanted to be able to do whatever I wanted, without having to ask. I thought I knew so much more than them. Do you know what I mean?" I don't say so, but I think I do.

"Then suddenly I was in that home with some really messed up kids. Let me tell you. There was a girl there who had burns up and down her back where her mother had put cigarettes out on her skin. There was a twelve-year-old girl who'd been sleeping on the streets for months because her father was molesting her. There were girls my age who could barely read and write, they'd spent so little time in school. And then there was me, messed up kid from the suburbs, whose parents never laid a finger on her, and who was just feeling sorry for herself. I was spoiled, Kat. *We* are spoiled. Let me tell you, 'cause I know."

I want to remind Hannah that she did some pretty mean things to me, so I wasn't entirely spoiled, but something tells me to let her talk.

"Then I knew I was going to have to tell someone that I was pregnant. I'd known for a while. It's one of the reasons I couldn't stand going to work at Tim Horton's. The smell made me sick. One of the girls at the home had had a baby when she was thirteen. I think she knew the minute she looked at me." Hannah stops talking and looks down at the squirrel. Its mate has scampered down the tree as well and is suspended at the bottom, its body upside down, all four paws grasping the bark.

"You don't know how scared I was the day I went to that clinic. You don't know how much I wished Mom could have been with me. Miss Kalputos said she'd call her for me, but I couldn't face her. Not after I'd called her all those names. It was so cold in that room. They only give you one of those thin hospital sheets to cover up. And even though they run the instruments under hot water, let me tell you they're cold, colder than ice, when they touch your skin.

"Afterwards, you bleed for a long time. You lie there and bleed. Lots of the other girls at the home had had abortions. There wasn't a lot of sympathy for me. I was so alone, Kat. You have no idea. I thought I might just lie there and bleed to death and never see anyone again. Lots of things were flushed out of me that day. Lots of things."

By the time Hannah finishes her speech, her chin is tucked so far inside the collar of her jacket that her face is almost swallowed. It's Hannah's turn to hide now, from me, from the world, even from the gaze of the squirrels who seem to be our only audience. My mind is racing to think up an appropriate response, but I don't know what tone to take. A few minutes ago anger seemed appropriate, but now I'm not sure. Should I show concern or sympathy? Neither of these feels natural, not in connection with Hannah anyway. I don't even know why Hannah is telling me all this. What does it have to do with me?

Suddenly, the two squirrels spin around and take off up the tree, into their winter hideaway. Hannah and I follow the creatures with our eyes. When the last inch of bushy gray tail has vanished into the hole, I ask Hannah, "Why are you telling me this?"

"Because, Kat. I want you to know. I know I was out of control. I think I know why, but that's another story. I wanted to do my own thing, you know? I felt I couldn't be the good girl that Dad wanted. You remember all those protest marches he took us on, all those fights against injustice? And the time we got tied to a tree? He had a way of making me feel I had to be so perfect. I had to be changing the world. Do you know that I lied and told him that I had started a social justice committee at school, when really it was a social committee? It's only a difference of one word. He thought I was planning rallies to help mothers in Nicaragua find their lost children, but really I was picking out music themes for dances and organizing fashion shows. I knew he'd be so disappointed if he found out."

"So it's Dad's fault?"

"That's not what I'm saying, Kat."

"And what does all that have to do with me?" I

try hard to remember that I was going to stay separate from other people. I don't want to be pulled in by explanations.

"After what you did today, you need to know. Trust me."

We continue to sit for a while, each wrapped in her own thoughts, until finally Hannah says, "We better go before they send the RCMP after me. I left a note that I was going shopping. We can walk home from here."

As we walk, Hannah stops a couple of times in front of various houses. She tells me these are some of the places where she delivered drugs in the summer. She stares up at one house intently, as though she expects to see a ghost of her former self emerge from the doorway and float down the front steps.

Our parents are in the front yard. My mother's pulling a long string of Christmas lights from a box, and my father's starting to climb the ladder that is braced against the sun porch wall. I take a deep breath. I can't be sure that Hannah won't tell. She did say when, not if, they find out. But I can't be sure. I can't be sure about anything right now. When my parents see us, they both stop what they're doing. It's like they're frozen in a snapshot. I catch the look of surprise on their faces. My father's mouth has even fallen open. My mother lets the lights slip from her mittens back into the box.

"Where've you been?" she asks as we step into the yard.

"Shopping," says Hannah. She looks at me and I hold my breath. "We ran into each other at the mall. Didn't we, Kat?" Hannah winks.

I simply nod. Then Hannah goes over to the base of the ladder that my father is standing on and steadies it with her feet.

Chapter 30

Later that night, I try to cram some information about the human body into my brain, but nothing sticks. Hannah's words keep replaying in my mind. I shake my head to erase them, but they're too persistent. I even put on my Diskman, hoping the music will drown out Hannah's voice, but it doesn't. Eventually I give up altogether and shut the book. It's then that I hear the sound. It seems to be coming from the heating shaft in the baseboard beside my bed. It's very faint, like gentle wind blowing through a crack in a window. I get down on all fours and plaster my ear to the grill. The sound comes in waves, stopping and starting at a steady rhythm.

It takes me a while, but I finally figure out what it is. It's the sound of crying. It must be Hannah. The sound must be entering the shaft in Hannah's new room, then travelling upwards through the system of old tin tunnels that branch out inside the walls like the nervous system I've been studying.

By the time the sobs reach my ears, they're barely more than a whisper.

I'm paralyzed. This isn't what I imagined. I remember hoping the new room would be like a cell and that Hannah would find every waking minute down there torture. I thought I'd take pleasure in Hannah's pain. But this is different. These are sobs of real intense sorrow and they make me tremble.

I picture Hannah under her new floral duvet, wrestling with memories that I only glimpsed in her speech this afternoon. And I think that even though the new room is as cheery as my parents could make it, it's still in the basement, behind the laundry room. Did Hannah take this to mean welcome back, but you're not completely in?

I don't know what to do with the knowledge that my sister is crying. Not telling on Hannah is an ingrained habit. So, I stick my head back in my biology book and try to study. My eyes glance over the summaries of the five systems: nervous, digestive, cardiovascular, respiratory and reproductive, but they mean nothing. There's a key system missing — one that can't be diagramed or molded into plastic parts. It's the system where emotions bubble and brew, like some witch's potion. It's the system that's now brimming over two floors below in the damp basement.

I wonder if my parents, wherever they are, can hear Hannah too. And if they can, will they go down and check on her? Is that something they would do now? After all, there were very few close and tender moments between Hannah and my parents in the year before she left. Hannah wasn't someone you hugged. She was someone you avoided.

Who would now take that first step forward?

It won't be me, not tonight, not even after everything Hannah did for me this afternoon. Besides, even if I could get down the stairs and into Hannah's new room, I wouldn't know what to say.

Or would I?

Hannah's sobbing has been going on for almost an hour. How much crying does she have to do? Is it just the abortion that she has to cry out of her system, or are there other things that I don't know about? Things that happened at the group home, or maybe even before it. Hannah was out of control for a long time, and I never stopped to wonder why. I was too busy staying out of her way.

Most of the lights downstairs are out and the house is quiet. I open the door to the basement and tiptoe down the stairs. I have no idea what I'm going to say. Perhaps Hannah will be angry that I'm interfering, or embarrassed to be caught crying. Hannah always wanted people to think she was tough. Maybe I should just turn around and mind my own business. That's what I intended to do after Hannah's return. Steer clear, ignore, pretend Hannah didn't exist.

At Hannah's closed door, I stop. I don't know whether to knock or just walk in. The knock might scare her, but at least it would warn her that someone is here. I opt for just opening the door quietly.

Hannah is curled up on her bed, her arms wrapped around her pillow. A hundred balls of scrunched up white tissues top the bedspread like snow.

"Hannah?"

Hannah sits up, startled.

"Are you okay?"

Hannah shrugs.

"I just wanted to tell you ... I wanted to tell you that I really like them."

Hannah looks bewildered. "Like what?"

"The earrings you made me. I really like them."

I take the earrings out of my pocket. I slip the hooks into the holes in my ears. It's the first time I've tried them on.

"See? Don't they look good?"

Hannah is just staring at the earrings. She must have waited weeks to get a word back through Miss Corvette, or Kalputos, or whatever, about whether her handiwork was appreciated, only to be met by silence. The earrings, I now know, were Hannah's way of apologizing.

"I especially like the feather. It's a nice touch. It makes them fly. See?" I swoosh my head around. The purple feathers flap around my chin. Hannah follows them with her red, puffy eyes.

"Well, I just wanted you to know," I say.

Hannah nods her head. "Thanks, Kat," she says faintly.

"And another thing ... I do remember." Hannah looks puzzled.

"The wumps, I mean." Hannah smiles.

"Oh ya, that. Goodnight, Kat."

"Goodnight."

I creep back upstairs to my room. I don't know why I'm so anxious to be quiet, as if I'm doing something wrong. Hiding my dealings with Hannah is just second nature, I guess. As I'm getting back into bed, I hear my parents' door opening. They must be going down to see Hannah. I lie there, listening for their footsteps on the stairs. I feel so torn. I'm actually glad, for Hannah's sake. But I also want to scream. What about me? Why don't they ever notice when I'm hurt? I picture them sitting on her bed and hugging her, then I see myself in that cold white room. I suddenly wish it had been my parents who came to fetch me. I would have liked them to see me sitting, completely numb, on that hard metal chair. This is who I am, I would have told them. See how cold and alone I look?

Someone is knocking at my door. Without waiting for an invitation, my parents enter.

"Hi, Kat," they say. I don't answer. I'm too shocked.

"It was really nice of you to go down and see Hannah," my mother says. Hannah. So, they're here to talk about Hannah. What a surprise! Then it dawns on me that Hannah may have told them about today. She seemed pretty certain at the park that they were going to find out. She would have had time at supper because I ate in my room again, with the door blocked.

"Kat ... we're sorry, you know." It's my father's

voice. "We didn't know what was going on. We know now that Hannah took a lot out on you. When we saw that bear …" His voice fades. He must mean Blackie, with the ripped paw. "We should've seen. Especially me, I should've seen. It's my job, isn't it?" My father hangs his head. Now I'm confused. I thought Hannah told my parents what I did. But maybe she told them what she did. My mind wanders to the ripped jean shirt. My bruises have healed, but the shirt is evidence. I could get it, but I'm not sure I need to.

"No, it was our job," my mother responds. "We both did poorly. We're going to try to do better, Kat. We're going to try to keep our eyes open this time." I see my mother stripping the dining room wallpaper and now I know what all that decorating was for — distraction. She was ripping with her eyes closed.

"If you have anything to tell us, you can, you know, Kat?" My father adds.

Maybe I should tell them. But it's hard to start talking when you're so used to hiding. But hiding got me nowhere, except smack into that horrible white office, I guess. I nod to show that I accept the offer. It's the best I can do for now.

"Well, goodnight, Kat," they both say together. I nod. Then they do something that completely stuns me. They bend down and hug me. I feel my whole body go stiff, as stiff as when I was sitting on the metal chair. I try to let my body go, to let it relax.

And, eventually, it does — a little.

Chapter 31

Monday morning, before the biology exam, I write the words "good luck" on a slip of paper and drop it onto Anita's lap. It's not the most articulate apology in the history of the human race, but it's better than nothing. *Nothing* is exactly what I'm expecting to accomplish on this exam as well. So much for the honour roll this year.

I look across the room at Andy, hoping to catch his eye before the exam starts. I owe him an apology too. But he's totally focused on his desk, probably running through all the information he and Jeff studied yesterday.

I let the exam sit on my desk for a few minutes before starting, then I pick up my pencil and fill in my name. That's probably the only question I'll get right. For the next ninety minutes, I work my way methodically from page to page. I know some of the answers are probably wrong; others I'm more sure of. None of my answers will be brilliant, but that's okay.

When the teacher calls out "Time" I run out of the classroom to catch Anita before break.

"Hi." I place myself right in front of her. "Listen, Anita, I'm sorry about yesterday. I was an idiot. I've been an idiot lately."

Anita just shrugs.

"I got caught, you know."

Anita's eyes widen and she finally looks up at me. "You did?"

"Ya."

"What happened?"

"Well, just what you said would happen. I got caught."

"Did they call the cops? Did they call your parents? You must have died. Are you grounded? My parents would kill me."

I almost chuckle. My parents are so different from Anita's. They probably won't ground me even when they do find out. I plan to tell them tonight, after supper. I can see my father leaning forward, fixing me with an intense look, and asking me to tell him all about it. He's always believed in talking, it's in his nature. We used to do a lot of it, but we just got out of the habit somehow. Maybe, after tonight, we'll start doing it again.

"No. Nothing like that. The store let me go with a warning. And my parents don't even know … yet."

"How could your parents not know?"

"Well, actually … Hannah rescued me."

"Hannah!?"

"Ya. Isn't that wild?"

"Well, sometimes help comes from strange places. Like, guess what? My mother is actually going to help me find my biological mother."

I gasp. "You're kidding!?"

"Nope. After I got home yesterday, I decided to just walk in and tell her. I guess you seemed so out of control in the store. I mean, you were stuffing everything into your pockets, Kat. It kind of scared me. I thought I never want to lose control like that, so I went home and decided that if I didn't tell my mother soon I might end up like you."

"Thanks a lot!"

"You know what I mean."

"Well, I'm glad that my stupidity was so inspiring for you."

We're standing right in front of the bathroom where I saw that horrible graffiti all those weeks ago. I have an urge to go inside and make up a new jingle, something like:

*The Kat Burglar's finished, her career's on
   the shelf*
*If you want something stolen, just take it
   yourself*

"Do you want to go outside? You can still have a cigarette. There's about five minutes left."

"No. Actually, I've decided to try to stop smoking. It's driving me crazy, I want one so bad, but I haven't smoked since yesterday, after I left the mall. What about you? Are you going to give up shoplifting?"

"I'll try. I mean, I want to," I answer unsurely. Anyway, now that Hannah knows about the shoplifting, it wouldn't be the same. It's not that I expect her to be monitoring me or anything, but she'd probably know. She's pretty good at sniffing out criminal activity. Besides, I felt as small and helpless as a mouse in that white room. I don't want to go through that again, ever, no matter how much of a thrill shoplifting gave me.

I ace the English exam in the afternoon, just like I thought I would. I have to read a short story about a poor black girl who goes home at lunch to find out that her family is being evicted from their apartment. That same day in school her teacher wants her to write a poem about something pretty that gives her pleasure in life, but she can't. She can only write about the eviction and the way she felt when she saw all her family's furniture heaped up on the sidewalk. The poem makes the teacher cry. I have to write about the theme of the story. That's pretty easy. It's about honesty. It's about the way you can't pretend to be happy when you have nothing to be happy about. Your emotions are completely controlled by what's going on around you, especially what's going on in your family.

I know this only too well.

The second part of the exam is to write either a

short composition or poem on the topic of mistakes. This is pretty easy too. It's not like I have to rack my brain to find examples.

Mistakes

A mistake will burrow inside you
like a squirrel in a tree

A mistake will haunt you
like wind in old vents

A mistake will cage you
like a broken bird

A mistake can't be torn away like old wallpaper
or pulled like a scarf from your sleeve

A mistake can't be pushed away
like a friend who's getting on your nerves

A mistake is something you have to face
like your image in a mirror

And confront
like a sister crying in the dark.

I smile at Mr. Curtis when he collects my exam. I'm sure he's going to love my poem. He winks as he adds my test to the pile. Mr. Curtis would be a good person to talk to, if I feel myself getting into trouble again. At least he's always shown an interest in listening. I guess Hannah feels that way about Miss Kalputos. Miss Kalputos really did help her, in the end. Hannah still has a lot of recovering to do, though. You don't cry like that if you're all better.

On the way home from school, I find Andy and lure him away from his pals.

"Hi, Andy. I just wanted to say I'm sorry about yelling at you yesterday. Let's just say it was a bad day. Maybe even the worst day of my life."

Andy looks confused. "Okay. Should I ask why?"

"No. Never mind. I might tell you sometime." I know I should tell Andy about the shoplifting. I mean, it's part of me now, isn't it?

We walk a block in silence.

"Andy, can I ask you a strange favour?"

He nods.

"That bird place you took me to. Could we go there again this weekend?"

"Sure."

"And … could we bring Hannah along?"

Andy's eyes widen. "Okay, if you want to."

"It's just that I think she'd really like it." I remember the sound of Hannah's weeping coming up from her own cage in the basement last night. "I think it would be good for her," I add.

But that's not the only reason I'd like to go. I see myself in the white room, rubbing my goose-pimpled arms. "And I think seeing the birds again will help me too."

I can't believe I'm saying this. It's the first time I've ever admitted needing help. And I can't believe that saying it makes me feel so good.

"You don't need to explain, " Andy says. "I know what effect those birds can have. Pretty powerful stuff!" Andy's free hand is swinging somewhere down around mine. Our gloved fingers keep brushing until finally a couple of them hook up.

As we walk toward home, I think about how I'm going to tell my parents that I got caught shoplifting. I know that telling them is the right thing to do, but it's not going to be easy. I'm really terrified. The pressure of Andy's fingers is the only thing giving me courage. That, and the memory of my parents' late-night apology.

"Well, maybe I'll see you later," Andy says.

"I hope so." He turns and starts to walk up toward his front door.

"Andy!" I hear my own voice, but it doesn't sound like me.

"Yeah?" Andy stops, then turns and comes back.

"I know it's been a bit ... strange lately. I guess maybe I've been a bit strange."

"You think maybe I hadn't noticed?" Andy smiles, and I think of all the times he has smiled at me just this way.

"I think it's going to get better now," I say. It's all I can think of saying.

Andy nods. He takes my hand again and

squeezes it. A moment later he winks, lets go and walks away.

My heart is pounding. I feel a tingle surge through my body, so much stronger than any feeling I ever had when I was lifting stuff.

The pathway to my house lies at my feet. When I get inside, I'm going to find Hannah and tell her about the birds.

I'll find a way to make her want to come see them.

I'll pull her there by the hand if I have to.